Dear Reader,

Home, family, comm[unity,] values we cherish m[ost ... They] ground us, comfort u[s ... us.] They certainly provide the perfect inspiration around which to build a romance collection that will touch the heart.

And so we are thrilled to have the opportunity to introduce you to the Harlequin Heartwarming collection. Each of these special stories is a wholesome, heartfelt romance imbued with the traditional values so important to you. They are books you can share proudly with friends and family. And the authors featured in this collection are some of the most talented storytellers writing today, including favorites such as Brenda Novak, Janice Kay Johnson, Jillian Hart and Patricia Davids. We've selected these stories especially for you based on their overriding qualities of emotion and tenderness, and they center around your favorite themes—children, weddings, second chances, the reunion of families, the quest to find a true home and, of course, sweet romance.

So curl up in your favorite chair, relax and prepare for a heartwarming reading experience!

Sincerely,

The Editors

PATRICIA DAVIDS

After thirty-five years as a nurse, Pat has hung up her stethoscope to become a full-time writer. She enjoys spending her new free time visiting her grandchildren, doing some long-overdue yard work and traveling to research her story locations. She resides with her husband in Wichita, Kansas. Pat always enjoys hearing from her readers. You can visit her on the web at www.patriciadavids.com.

HARLEQUIN HEARTWARMING

Patricia Davids

Balancing Act

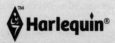

TORONTO NEW YORK LONDON
AMSTERDAM PARIS SYDNEY HAMBURG
STOCKHOLM ATHENS TOKYO MILAN MADRID
PRAGUE WARSAW BUDAPEST AUCKLAND

Recycling programs
for this product may
not exist in your area.

ISBN-13: 978-0-373-36438-1

BALANCING ACT

Copyright © 2011 by Patricia Macdonald

Originally published as LOVE THINE ENEMY
© 2006 by Patricia Macdonald

Printed in U.S.A.

Balancing Act

With endless thanks to my critique partners,
Deborah and Theresa. You girls rock!
So many words—so little paper.

Chapter One

Cheryl Steele planted her hands on her hips. "Angie, in order to attend your wedding, I have endured the wrath of my director, risked losing the best role of my career and traveled miles out of my way. At this moment, I'm very close to regretting all that effort."

In the small dressing room at the back of an old stone church on the outskirts of Wichita, Kansas, Cheryl's sister ignored her ire. "You will go out to the ranch, won't you? For me?" Angie coaxed again. "It's practically on your way."

"It's fifty miles *out* of my way." Exasperated

by her younger sibling's persistence, Cheryl tried changing the subject. "Your veil isn't straight. Let me fix it."

"My veil is fine. You didn't answer my question."

"Yes, I did. Two dozen times in the past two days. The answer is *no!* Now, hush." Cheryl adjusted the veil then stepped back and gazed in poignant wonder at the vision in satin and lace before her.

"Well?" Angie demanded.

"You look…radiant…beautiful…. I don't think I can find the right words. Jeff is a lucky man. I hope he knows it."

A mischievous grin curved Angie's lips. "He does. I tell him every chance I get."

Cheryl chuckled. "I bet you do."

Angie's smile faded. "Please say you will go out to the ranch before you leave the state. For me. Consider it a wedding present."

Cheryl sighed. "You don't give up, do you?"

"Not when it's important."

"There's nothing important about a few acres of grass and some rundown buildings in the middle of nowhere."

"It was our home. Our family is there."

"No! It was never a home after Mom died!" Cheryl shouted, then realized she was overreacting. She drew a deep breath and tried for a calmer tone. "I'm sorry. That ranch was the place we were stuck at until Cousin Harriet took us away. *She* gave us a home, and *you* are all the family I have left."

Irritated by her sister's persistence, Cheryl turned away and busied herself with the satin ribbons of Angie's bouquet of fragrant yellow roses. "I don't know why you keep harping on the subject."

"Harriet wanted you to go back, Cheryl. It was the last thing she asked of you before she died."

"I know." Cheryl's anger drained away, replaced with an aching sense of loss. She owed everything to Harriet Steele.

The day their mother's cousin had descended like a whirlwind to defy their grandmother and whisk both girls away from the ranch had been like something out of a fairy tale. At first, Cheryl had been terrified their grandmother would come and take them back. But after a month in Philadelphia,

Harriet had called Cheryl and Angie into her study and told them they were to live with her for as long as they liked. She had granted them an opportunity of a lifetime—a chance to live where no one knew them—where no one looked down on them.

And she gave Cheryl an even greater gift— the opportunity to study ballet. Harriet had passed away five years ago, a month before Cheryl debuted in her first major role, but Cheryl knew that every step she danced, every triumph she achieved in her career, she owed directly to that staunch, remarkable woman. Knowing that she had failed to honor the woman's last request left a bruised place in her heart.

Cheryl glanced at her sister's troubled face. This was Angie's wedding day. She should be happy today. She deserved that and much more.

"Why is it so important to you?"

"Because I see that you need closure, even if you won't admit it. You're still hiding. You're still afraid, and it isn't healthy."

"I'm not afraid." Somehow, her words didn't carry the conviction she had hoped for.

"Then you'll go?"

"No."

"Not even for me?"

With her sister's disappointment so painfully clear, Cheryl found herself wavering. "It's not like Doris would welcome me with open arms. Besides, if she didn't care enough to come to your wedding, why should I make an effort to see her?"

"Grandma Doris is stuck in the past. She can't…or won't…move on with her life. Seeing you, perhaps gaining your forgiveness, it could help. As for Jake—"

"Stop it!" Cheryl's anger came roaring back to life and she cut her sister off with a raised hand. "I don't want to hear another word about those people. Not one word!"

Angie caught Cheryl in an unexpected quick hug. "Oh, Cheryl, where we come from is part of what makes us who we are. Changing your name didn't change that."

"Now you sound like a psychologist."

Drawing back with a little laugh, Angie said, "That's because I'm studying to become one, remember?"

"I thought you were going to treat kids.

I'm twenty-six years old, sis. Four years older than you."

Sadness settled over Angie's features. "You may be older, but in some ways you are still a hurting little girl. I would go back and change things if I could. So much of it was my fault."

Cheryl took her sister's face between her hands. "Don't ever say that. The blame belongs to Dad and Jake and Doris. They were the adults. You were a child."

"You were a child, too."

"I was old enough to know what I was doing. I don't regret anything."

"If that were true, you wouldn't have cut yourself off from Grandma Doris and Jake after Dad died. You can't let unresolved issues from the past ruin your life."

Cheryl looked at Angie in amazement. "Are you kidding? My life isn't ruined. I'm the lead ballerina in a fabulous dance company. What more could I want?"

"But are you happy?"

Was she? She was happy when she danced, but after the lights went down…when she went home to an empty apartment alone… Cheryl shook off the troubling thoughts.

"Hey, I'm supposed to be asking you that question. You're the one getting married."

Angie's expression softened. "I'm very happy. I am blessed in more ways than I can count. I am thankful every day. I have even found my true love."

Determined to sidetrack Angie's questions, Cheryl said, "I do wish you and Jeff could come see me dance. It's a wonderful production of *Alice in Wonderland,* and I *love* the role of Alice. Our performance tonight is a special one for disadvantaged children. That was one reason I really wanted the role. Most of the cities on our tour have at least one performance especially for children. You know I believe kids everywhere should have a chance to see how beautiful ballet is.

"I wish we could have worked it out, too. But that silly man of mine wants to take me to Hawaii for our honeymoon. Who am I to argue with a romantic like that?"

"All right. If I can't talk you out of marrying the fool, then let's get started so I can get on the road. The forecast is calling for snow. Snow in April! I'd almost forgotten how unpredictable the weather is out here. I'll never understand why you moved back."

"I came back because this is where my roots are. Yours are here, too."

"No, mine have been transplanted to New York, and they're thriving, thank you very much."

Angie studied Cheryl's face for a long second. "I wish I believed that."

"Enough with the analyzing."

"You can't keep avoiding the subject forever."

"I can, and I will. Drop it, Angela. I mean it. I don't have any family except you. That's the way it is."

"What if Jake asked to see you?"

"I'd say, 'Jake who?'"

"He's your brother."

"Half brother."

Angie reached out and took hold of Cheryl's hand. "Can't you consider forgiving him?"

"No. He got what he deserved and Eldorado Prison is *not* on my itinerary—so don't even ask."

Angie's shoulders slumped and she nodded in resignation. A knock sounded at the door and she went to open it. One of the ushers stood on the other side.

"Everything's ready," he said. "The guitarist wants to know if he should start playing or if you wanted to see him first."

Angie looked at Cheryl and sighed. She turned back to the usher. "Tell him to start playing, please."

Cheryl didn't understand the sorrow in her sister's voice. "What's the matter, honey?"

Angie held out her hand. "Why is it that the people I love are all so stubborn? Never mind. Let's go get me married."

Hours later, hunched over the steering wheel of her rental car, Cheryl peered through snowflakes the size of goose feathers as they filled the beams of her headlights. She was driving into a storm and into the middle of nowhere, and for what? Because she couldn't bear to remember the look of disappointment on her sister's face.

Tightening her grip on the wheel, Cheryl marveled at her own folly in leaving the turnpike for this deserted stretch of rural highway. She had a major performance later tonight. She should be resting in her hotel room by now. But when the exit sign for Highway 77 had appeared, she had taken it—almost against her will. That had been an hour ago—long enough to regret her decision a hundred times. Still, she had to be close now. She fought down the feeling of dread that rose with the thought. Seconds later, the gray shape of a rural mailbox loomed out of the snowy night.

She braked, feeling the car slide on the slick road as she turned into the barely discernable country lane and stopped.

At least the snow and the darkness hid the desolate landscape of the rolling Flint Hills from her sight. Only a dim gleam, from a porch light or perhaps a window, showed her where the old ranch house stood out on the prairie. She was home.

No sense of nostalgia filled her—only bitterness—a bitterness buried so deep she hadn't realized she still carried it until this moment. Staring at the flickering light in the distance, she suddenly understood why she had come.

She hadn't come because of Angie's pleadings. She had come to prove that nothing remained of the frightened girl who had left so many years ago.

"You can't hurt me anymore!" She wanted to shout those words in the old woman's face, but she didn't move. Her fingers grew ice-cold where she gripped the wheel as the old shame and fears crawled back to replace her bravado.

Coming here had been a mistake. She shifted the car into Reverse. She couldn't change the past. No one could. Cheryl Thatcher had effectively buried that past. Cheryl Steele didn't intend to resurrect it. Angie might believe in forgiveness, in healing old wounds, but Cheryl didn't. There was no forgiveness in this bleak land.

The tires whined as they spun in the snow, then suddenly they caught and the car lurched out of the lane and onto the pavement. Cheryl shifted into Drive, then stepped on the gas and didn't look back as she headed down the winding two-lane highway that would take her away. This time, forever.

Half an hour later, she raged at her own stupidity and bad luck. The snow came down faster and thicker with every mile. Her side trip had turned into a major mistake. A glance at the clock on her dash showed it was already half-past six. It would be close, but she could still make it. She *had* to. Her position was too important to risk by missing a performance. She would have to let Damon know she was running late. She dreaded placing the call. He wasn't an easy man to deal with at the best of times. Reaching down, she fumbled in her purse for her cell phone.

"Dumb cow," Sam Hardin muttered under his breath. "I try to do you a favor and this is the thanks I get. You make me ride home in the dark."

He glanced across the corral to the long, low shed where his cattle huddled together out of the wind. One stubborn heifer had refused to join the herd and had kept Sam searching for her long after the others were rounded up. He swung the metal gate shut with a clang after she ambled through. Now all his expectant cows and those with newborn calves at their sides were safe from the approaching storm. He dismounted to make sure the gate was secure, then leaned his arms on the top panel.

The truth was he didn't mind the ride or the time alone. He didn't have a reason to hurry home tonight. No one would be missing him. His grandfather might be up pretending to watch television while he dozed in his chair, but the twins were spending the night with Sam's mother, and without the girls' constant activity and chattering voices, the big house felt empty and lonely. As empty as his heart had felt since Natalie left him.

Beside him, his bay gelding snorted and shook his head. Drops of melting snow flew from his long mane, and his bridle jingled faintly in the cold air. Sam left off his somber musing and gathered the reins as he cast a worried look at the sky.

"I guess that stockman's advisory is going to be right on the money, tonight, Dusty," he said in disgust. "When was the last time it snowed like this in April?"

Mounting, Sam turned his horse for home. It was dark and snowing heavily by the time he reached the main pasture gate. He dismounted, opened it and led Dusty out, then he stretched the barbed wire strands taut and lowered the wire hoop over the gatepost. He turned his coat collar up against the rising wind and settled his hat more firmly on his head.

Remounting, he patted Dusty's neck and spoke to the patient cow pony. "Only a little longer, fella. Then you can bed down in a warm stall with an extra ration of oats— you've earned it."

Dusty's ears perked at the mention of oats, and Sam laughed softly as he set his horse into a trot along the wide shoulder of the highway and headed for the ranch house. Suddenly, the glare of headlights blinded him as a car sped out of the snowy night and came straight at him.

At the last second, the car swerved, then pitched into a skid on the icy roadway. From the corner of his eye, Sam saw the vehicle fly past as his horse leapt sideways. It missed them by inches as it spun off the road, plunged down an embankment and slammed to a stop in a small group of trees.

Sam reined in his terrified horse. It had been a close call—too close. The thought of his daughters losing another parent sent a chill up his spine that had nothing to do with the temperature.

With his heart still hammering wildly, Sam dismounted and stared at the car in the ditch. *Please, let everyone be okay.*

He left his horse at the edge of the road and made his way down the steep slope to the wrecked car. His boots slipped in the wet snow, and he skidded the last few feet to the bottom. He saw the driver's door was crushed against a cedar tree, so Sam made his way to the opposite side. What kind of idiot drove at such breakneck speed in this weather, anyway? He yanked open the passenger door and the dome light came on.

The idiot was a woman. Her blond head rested against the high seat back with her pale face half turned toward him. A thin line of blood trickled from her left temple, slipped down the slender column of her throat and disappeared beneath the scooped neckline of her red sweater.

Was she dead? The grim thought sent a curl of dread through him. He jerked off his gloves and leaned in to check for a pulse.

He found one, strong and steady beneath his fingers. Relieved, he let out a breath he hadn't realized he was holding. Her eyes fluttered opened, and she blinked in the light.

"Lady, are you okay?" he asked, trying to sound calm.

She lifted a shaky hand to her head. "I don't think so."

Bitter-cold air swept around Sam and into the car as he held the door open. Her trembling was probably due to shock and not the freezing temperature, but he wasn't helping. Easing onto the slanting front seat, he closed the door. The interior light shut off, and the only illumination came from the headlights reflecting off the snow outside. He began to unknot the bandanna at his throat. "Where are you hurt?"

"I'm going to be so late," she muttered and closed her eyes.

Fright and cold made his fingers clumsy. With a jerk, the bandanna finally came loose. He pressed it to her bleeding temple. "Late for your own funeral, maybe. You're crazy to be driving so fast in this weather."

She pushed his hand away and turned a

fierce scowl in his direction. "I'm not the crazy one here! You were riding a horse in the middle of a highway—at night—in a snowstorm! Do you have a death wish?" she shouted, then winced.

"Lady, I wasn't in the middle of the highway. I was on the shoulder when you came barreling at me. The road curves here, but I guess you didn't notice. You were over the center line and speeding toward the ditch. I just happened to be in your way."

She stared at him a long moment. "Oh."

"Yeah, oh!"

"Well, I missed you, didn't I?"

The last of his tension evaporated. "You did. You have my sincere thanks for that. If you'd gone off the other side of this curve at the speed you were traveling you might be dead now. There's a steep drop and a stone wall on that side."

He offered the bandanna again. "Are you hurt anywhere besides that cut on your forehead?"

"I'm not sure." Taking the cloth from him, she held it to her head and gave a hiss of pain. After a second, she focused on him again.

Sudden tears welled up in her eyes. "I'm so sorry. Are you sure you're okay? Is your horse all right?"

"Dusty and I are fine, honest."

"It all happened so fast. I almost killed you." A sob escaped as a tear slipped down her pale cheek.

"*Almost* doesn't count except in horseshoes and hand grenades. Hey, yelling I can take, but tears—don't even go there," he warned.

She managed a trembling half smile. "I'll try."

Sam shot a quick look at the windshield. The wipers had stopped with the engine, and snow already covered the glass.

"We need to get out of this weather, and this car isn't going anywhere. My ranch isn't far, but we should get going before this storm gets any worse. Can you move?"

"I think so." She shifted in the seat, then gave a sharp cry as she grabbed her left thigh with both hands.

"What's wrong?"

"My foot is caught," she answered through clenched teeth.

He saw a tremor race through her body.

The temperature inside the car was dropping rapidly. He needed to get her someplace warm and soon.

"Here, take my coat while I have a look." He shrugged out of his sheepskin jacket and tucked it around her shoulders. They felt slender and fragile under his large, work-hardened hands. Her hair swept across the back of his wrist in a soft whisper stirring an unexpected awareness of her as a woman. He forced the thought to the back of his mind. He needed to concentrate on getting her out of here.

She bit her lip as she tried again to move. "My foot's wedged under something. I can't move it, and it hurts when I try."

Reaching over the steering column, he turned on the interior light. "Hold still while I check it out." Leaning down, he peered under the dash. "I'm Sam Hardin, by the way."

Cheryl's breath caught in a sharp gasp of surprise. He was one of the high-and-mighty Hardins. Her pulse began to pound. Feelings of shame and guilt rose like bile in the back of her throat. This couldn't be happening. Not now, not after all this time.

She glanced fearfully at the man beside her. Did he know who she was? Had he seen her family's pictures plastered across the local papers? Had he been at the trial that had sent her father and brother to prison? Did he know she had been her father's accomplice and that she'd done time for her crime?

Chapter Two

Cheryl drew a shaky breath and forced herself to calm down. Of course Sam Hardin didn't know who she was. How could he? It had all happened nearly fifteen years ago. She wasn't a child anymore; she was an adult now. Driving by the old ranch had dredged up painful feelings and the accident had unnerved her, that was all.

"I'm pleased to meet you, Mr. Hardin. My name is Cheryl Steele," she said at last, watching his reaction. She'd changed her name when she was old enough, wanting to be rid of even that reminder of her childhood.

Only a handful of people knew she had once been Cheryl Thatcher.

"Pleased to meet you, Cheryl Steele, and you can call me Sam. So where are you from? That's an East-Coast accent I hear, isn't it?"

"Manhattan," she confirmed, relaxing even more. It was true. The city had been her home for the past six years.

"You're from Manhattan, Kansas?" he asked from under the dash.

"No, Manhattan, New York," she said quickly. Something was wrong, seriously wrong. She tried but still couldn't budge her foot. Fiery agony shot up her leg. "The pain's getting worse."

"Okay, hold still while I see if I can move this metal."

"Hurry, please."

"You're a long way from home, New York. What are you doing way out here?"

"I thought I was taking a shortcut to Manhattan."

"You were taking a shortcut to New York City on this road?" he asked, his amusement evident.

"Very funny," she muttered in annoyance.

"No, not a shortcut to *the* Manhattan. I'm trying to get *your* Manhattan. I need to be at the University Theater by seven at the latest. It's very important."

Her whole foot throbbed painfully now. She had to perform in less than an hour. She couldn't be trapped out here.

He grunted with effort as he tried to move the crumpled metal. "It gave a little. Try now."

Her foot wouldn't budge. Panic swelled in her and she struggled against the confining metal. "Please, get me out of here!"

"I will. Take it easy."

"I'm a ballet dancer," she whispered. What if her injury was serious? What if she couldn't dance? Didn't he understand how frightened she was?

He sat up beside her. Softly, he cupped her cheek with one hand and wiped a tear away with his thumb. "You'll be dancing again in no time, New York. Right now we have to keep our heads. Your foot is caught between the floor and the side wall where it's caved in. I'll get you out, but it may take a bit."

She managed a nod. "Okay. I understand."

"Thatta girl."

Cheryl worked to regain control of her emotions. He was right. She had to keep her head. She needed to focus on something besides the fear and the pain. She had learned that trick early in life and used it often in her grueling career. She chose his face.

His rugged features softened when he smiled. It made the creases in his lean cheeks deepen and small crinkles appear at the corner of his eyes. His mouth lifted a little higher on one side, giving his smile a roguish charm.

Suddenly, she was grateful to have him in the dimness beside her. His hand was gentle when he'd touched her face. His voice was calm and steady. He inspired trust, and that thought surprised her. For most of her life she had considered ranchers to be the enemy—something else she had learned early on.

He said, "I need to find a way to pry this metal apart."

"There should be a jack in the trunk," she volunteered.

"Good thinking." He flashed her a big,

heart-stopping, crooked grin. "Kinda smart for a city girl, aren't you?"

His teasing comment amused her even though she suspected he was simply trying to distract her from the seriousness of the situation. Well, she could play city-girl versus country-boy, too. After all, she was a rising star with the New York Theater Ballet. She had performed far more difficult roles.

"I don't imagine you keep a jack in your saddle-bags, cowboy. Or do you?" she quipped.

"No, ma'am, I don't." He slipped into an exaggerated drawl that would have done a Texan proud. "My ol' hoss has gone lame, but he ain't never gone flat."

Cheryl tried not to smile at his poor joke.

Pulling the keys from the ignition, he grinned as he opened the car door. "I'll be back in a jiffy."

She nodded, but she had to fight another wave of panic as the door closed behind him, leaving her alone. She took several deep breaths until she felt in control of her emotions. A glance out the windshield told her what she already knew. She was going to miss tonight's performance.

Her understudy would be able to dance the part, but Damon Sands, their director, was going to be furious. He'd already been unhappy about Cheryl's plans to leave the company during their short break to travel to her sister's wedding. Only her repeated assurances that she'd be back in plenty of time for the production had mollified him. Now, she'd be lucky if she didn't lose her position after this fiasco. Damon had an unforgiving nature, especially when it came to his work.

She searched around for her cell phone but couldn't find it. Moments before the wreck she had tried to use her phone only to see that it displayed No Signal. Chances were it wouldn't work even if she had it in her hand. She was stuck with no way of letting Damon know where she was.

Stuck in the middle of nowhere, that's where she was. No, worse. She was stuck in the middle of the Flint Hills. Until two months ago, nothing could have induced her to return here. Nothing, that was, until the call from Angie. Even as she'd listened to her sister's deliriously happy voice begging her to come for the wedding, Cheryl had hesitated. She'd given in to her sister's pleading only because the wedding would be in Wichita. A hundred miles seemed far enough away from their old home to let her feel safe about a brief visit.

Yet, even with this catastrophe, Cheryl was glad she had come. She smiled as she remembered the beautiful ceremony in the tiny church decorated with ivy and deep yellow roses. The strains of a classical guitar floating down from the choir loft had filled the air with the sounds of love transformed into music.

A blast of cold air jerked her back to the present as Sam opened the car door and slipped in beside her. Working quickly, he positioned the jack and after several turns, the metal pinning her began to spread. He eased her foot loose and she bit her lip to keep from crying out at the pain.

"I'm sorry if I hurt you," he said.

Unable to speak, she nodded. Her foot throbbed wildly.

"At least you're free." His bright tone made her want to hit him.

"Can you ride a horse, New York?"

Her gaze flew to his. "You're kidding, right?" One look told her he wasn't. She nearly groaned at the idea of hanging her leg over a horse.

"Of course I can ride," she answered with more confidence than she felt. She hadn't been near a horse in fifteen years.

"Good, I'd hate for this to be your first lesson. Do you have a coat or something to keep you warm? The wind is bitter outside."

"It's on the backseat."

He retrieved it for her. After returning his coat, Cheryl slipped into her own, then located her purse on the floor. She gritted her teeth as she prepared to leave the relative safety of the car.

Sam stepped out and pulled on his coat, glad of its retained warmth. Thick snow swirled past his face. Glancing up, he saw Dusty standing at the edge of the road with his head down and his rump to the wind. A whistle brought the horse to him, and Sam turned to Cheryl. He grinned at the expression on her face as she stared at Dusty. "Don't worry, New York, I won't let you fall off."

"I'm not worried about falling off, cowboy. I'm worried about freezing solid up there," she shot back.

"Freeze on the horse, be home in thirty minutes and thaw out in a hot bath, or freeze in the car and wait for the next taxi to come by. It's your choice."

"When you put it that way..." She sent him a suspicious look. "A hot bath—you promise?"

"Yup. Cross my heart."

He swung up into the saddle and offered her his hand. She jumped as he lifted her and swung her up behind him. To his surprise, she made the move with ease and grace. He glanced back at her face and saw her lips pressed into a hard, tight line, but she didn't complain. Miss New York had guts, all right. She settled her hands at his hips, but he pulled her arms tight around his waist.

It felt good. It felt right. It had been a long time since a woman had held him.

He turned the horse toward home, glad he

had two long snow-covered miles to remind himself she was an injured woman who needed his care, nothing more. She was only passing through.

The elegant dancer behind him might stir his senses, but he wasn't foolish enough to act on that attraction. He certainly wasn't looking to get involved with any woman again. Not after Natalie. He would never give another woman the power to hurt him or his children the way his ex-wife had.

Cheryl clung to Sam and kept her face pressed to his back, but soon, even his large, powerful frame offered little comfort. Her head and her leg throbbed with every step the horse took. The wind chilled her to the bone, and there was nothing she could do except endure it. That was how she remembered this country. As something to be endured.

"How much farther?" she yelled over the wind. Her purse strap slipped off her shoulder and slid down her arm to bump against the horse's side, but she didn't loosen her grip to pull it up as she huddled behind Sam.

"Not much. Less than half a mile," he shouted back.

In spite of his encouragement, it seemed like hours before the horse finally stopped. Lifting her aching head, Cheryl saw they stood in front of a small porch surrounded by a wooden railing already piled high with snow. Snow-laden cedars stood on either side of the porch hiding most of the pale, native limestone house from her view, but the warm glow of the porch light was as welcome as all the bright lights of Broadway.

She released her frozen grip on Sam. He swung his leg forward over the horse's neck and slid down. Turning, he lifted her off the horse and lowered her gently to the ground. Balancing on one foot, she clung to his shoulders. Then, without a word, he swept her up into his arms.

She wrapped her hands around his neck, and her gaze moved to his face. She became aware of the strength in the arms that held her and the intensity of his gaze as he studied her in return. Suddenly, she felt warm and breathless.

An echo of that awareness flared in his eyes. Then, just as quickly, his gaze cooled. "Let's get you inside."

Sam forced his attention away from the sweet, soft curve of her lips. He quickly climbed the steps, wrestled one-handed with the door, then stepped inside. After setting his guest gently on the high-backed bench in the entry, he took in her battered appearance.

She was as pale as the snow outside. Streaks of dried blood ran from a bruised cut on her temple down the left side of her face and neck. Blond hair, slightly longer than shoulder length, framed her face in soft waves. Her eyes were a startling sapphire-blue surrounded by thick, dark blond lashes. But when she looked up at him, he saw pain and exhaustion filling them. The total sum of her fragile beauty stunned him like the kick of a horse.

"Are you okay?" he managed to ask.

She nodded. "I just need to warm up."

"Rest here. I have to put Dusty away. I'll be back in a few minutes." He started out the door, then turned. "Oh, watch out for the cat. He's Bonkers."

She glanced around, then closed her eyes with a grimace as she leaned her head back.

"Crazy cowboy owns an insane cat. Why doesn't that surprise me?"

Chuckling, Sam left the house and quickly led Dusty to the barn. He unsaddled the horse, fed him a measure of grain and gave him a fast rubdown.

"So, what do you think of her?" he asked. Dusty kept his nose buried in his oats. Sam paused in his brushing. "What, no comment? It's not every day an ugly old cow pony gets to give a real ballerina a ride. Me—I think she's drop-dead gorgeous."

Dusty snorted once. Sam grinned and resumed the quick, short strokes of his brush. "You're right, looks aren't everything. I'll put her up for the night, then get her out of here first thing tomorrow." He gave the horse a final pat and left.

Pausing outside the barn door, Sam turned up the collar of his coat. The blowing snow piled in growing drifts around the barn. If this storm didn't let up soon, he could be stuck with his unexpected guest for more than one night. The idea didn't annoy him the way it should have. Instead, a strange feeling of anticipation grew as he started toward the house.

The sound of the door opening and a gust of frigid air announced Sam's return. Cheryl eyed her rescuer closely as he paused inside the entry to hang up his coat and hat. As he raked a hand though his dark brown hair, curls flattened by his hat sprang back to life, and she noticed a touch of gray at his temples. He was older than she'd first thought. Perhaps somewhere in his early thirties.

As he turned toward her, she guessed he had to be six foot two at least. He towered over her, but he wasn't intimidating. His eyes were warm and friendly. A rich hazel color, they were framed with thick, dark lashes any woman would envy. He didn't have a classically handsome face, she thought, yet there was something appealing about it.

She gave herself a swift mental shake. What on earth was wrong with her? She had more sense than to be moonstruck by a handsome man with a pair of smiling eyes. Plus, he was a rancher. *And* a Hardin. She'd seen enough of that judgmental and unforgiving lot in her youth to last her two lifetimes. The chiming of a clock sent her thoughts back to her real problem.

"Thanks for the rescue, cowboy, but I can't stay."

"My granddad lives with me if you're worried about your reputation."

"It's not that. I have to get to Manhattan."

"You aren't going anywhere tonight."

"It's important."

"Unless you can change the weather or sprout wings and fly, you're stuck."

She sighed in defeat. "May I use a telephone? I lost my cell phone in the car. I have to let someone know what's happened to me."

"There's a phone in the living room," he said, stooping to gather her in his arms again.

"I can make it on my own," she protested.

"Not till I see how bad that leg is." He swept her up effortlessly, carried her into the living room, and set her gently on the sofa. Bending over her leg, he eased off her shoe and sock.

A hiss of pain escaped Cheryl's clenched lips, and her hands grew white-knuckled as she gripped the sofa cushions.

He let out a slow whistle. "Lady, you aren't going be dancing on this anytime soon. You need X-rays, maybe even a cast. I'll get some ice for it. That may keep some of the swelling down."

Cheryl opened her eyes when the pain receded and stole a quick peek at her throbbing foot. Her ankle, discolored and swollen, looked as bad as it felt, but she'd danced on worse. Her art demanded it.

With her career in mind, she glanced around for the phone, then paused as she caught sight of her surroundings. For a moment, she felt as Alice might have when she stepped through the looking glass. The small porch flanked by cedars had given her the wrong impression. Instead of an old farmhouse, she found herself in a home that looked like a color layout for *Better Homes and Gardens.* A series of floor-to-ceiling windows made up one entire wall of the huge room. To her right, a wide staircase led down to a lower level, and to her left was an open, airy country kitchen.

A bold Indian-blanket pattern covered the sofa she rested on. Its brick-red, hunter-green and royal-blue tones were reflected in the room's brightly colored accents. Matching love seats flanked the sofa and formed a cozy seating area arranged at the edge of a large, patterned rug. Polished wooden floors and a rough beam ceiling lent added warmth to the room.

Looking over the open counter into the kitchen, she watched Sam move deftly, getting ice, a plastic bag and a towel. He seemed at home in the kitchen. That didn't exactly fit the rugged cowboy images she remembered.

He returned and handed her a small ice bag. "For that bump on your head."

"Thank you." Cheryl took the bag and held it to her temple. He placed a second pack carefully around her ankle.

For such a big man, he had gentle hands. She shivered when he touched her bare skin. Abruptly, she pulled her foot away. "I can manage."

Her rapid heart rate had to be from the pain and nothing else. "You have a fabulous home," she said to distract him when he shot her a puzzled look.

"You were expecting a dilapidated log

cabin?" An engaging sparkle glinted in the depths of his eyes.

"Oh, not in Kansas." Her reply was quick and flippant. "Everyone knows there aren't any trees out here. I was expecting a soddy."

"A soddy?" His eyebrows shot up in surprise. "I'm impressed you know the term. Sorry to disappoint you, New York. We don't live in sod houses anymore."

"Don't tell me you have electricity and indoor plumbing, too?" she asked in mock amazement.

He stood and grinned at her. "Smart aleck. Make your phone calls. I'll let Granddad know we have a guest for the night."

Cheryl worried briefly that his grandfather might be someone who would recognize her, but her other concerns pushed the worry aside. She had more pressing problems. She picked up the phone and punched in Damon's cell phone number. When he finally answered, he had little sympathy for her dilemma.

"This tour is a showcase of my work. A second-rate dancer can make it look second-rate. How can you do this to me?"

"I'm sorry, Damon. It was an accident. I'll

catch up with you as soon as I can get another rental car."

"How bad is your foot?" he asked with grudging concern.

"Only a sprain. It'll be fine in a few days."

"I hope so. I don't need to remind you that good reviews mean good attendance, and good attendance means better funding for the company. If this tour doesn't go well, we'll all be looking for work."

"I know. I'll be there as soon as I can."

"Two days! We open in Kansas City in two days. Don't let me down, Cheryl. Work is hard to find when word gets out that a dancer is unreliable."

It was a threat—one she didn't dare ignore. She was on her way up in her career, but Damon Sands could make things hard for her if he chose.

"I'll be there," she promised. Nothing was going to keep her from finishing this tour.

"You'd better be," he snapped and hung up.

The last call she placed went to the rental car company. They weren't happy with her, either. She'd just finished that conversation when Sam walked back into the room.

"You're looking kind of glum, New York. Is your boyfriend mad at you for standing him up?"

She pressed her fingers to her throbbing temples. "My boss, not my boyfriend, and, yes, he's angry. This tour is important to him, and to me."

"Tour?" he asked, clearly puzzled.

"I dance, remember? My ballet company is on an eight-city tour for the spring. We've been performing in Tulsa for the past two weeks. We were scheduled to give a one-night-only performance at the University Theater in Manhattan tonight. From there, we go on to Kansas City for a week, then two weeks in Denver, two weeks in Salt Lake City, then Reno, Fresno and San Francisco."

"How'd you get separated from your company?"

"That is a long story."

"I'm not going anywhere and neither are you," he said, sitting beside her.

He was right. She tried to keep the bitterness out of her voice as she recounted the tale that had landed her almost in his lap. Literally.

"My sister called a few months ago to tell me she was getting married. She knew I'd be on this tour, so we planned her wedding to coincide with a break in my itinerary. The wedding was today."

"Your sister lives near here?"

"In Wichita. We had it all planned," Cheryl said with a shake of her head. "I flew from Tulsa to Wichita for the wedding. I couldn't get a flight into Manhattan today so I rented a car. The rest you know."

She pushed back a strand of hair and sighed. "My company will travel to Kansas City tomorrow with or without me."

She wouldn't think about what would happen if she couldn't join them—if her foot was broken, not just sprained, and she couldn't work for weeks.

"We can't do anything about it tonight," Sam said.

He was right. She would simply have to make the best of it.

"I doubt the road to Manhattan is even open now," Sam continued. "Soon as the weather clears, I'll get you to Kansas City even if we have to ride Dusty all the way."

The twinkle in his eyes proved he was trying to cheer her. She held up her hands clasped together and begged, "Not that! Please! Not another ride on Dusty."

"Now, that will hurt his feelings."

"Not as much as he hurt my behind."

Cheryl gazed at Sam's amused face feeling oddly happy in spite of her predicament. It was easy to trade banter with him. Why was that? He was everything that she had loathed, once upon a time.

Still smiling, he stood and held out his hand. "Come on. I've got the perfect answer for your saddle sores. I ran a bath for you while you were on the phone."

She brightened. "That's right. You did promise me a hot bath to get me to come home with you."

"And you accepted, cheap date that you are." He picked her up, and she circled his neck with her arms.

Her pulse began to race once more, and she didn't try to delude herself—it wasn't due to the pain in her foot. She tried for a nonchalant tone. "Obviously, I need to raise my standards. Next time you'll have to promise me chocolate and roses."

His gaze met hers for a long instant. "It's a deal," he said softly. She looked away first.

He carried her through a doorway beyond the kitchen and through a huge bedroom to the bath. The room, tiled in stark black and white, held a large, black whirlpool tub in one corner, while a separate shower area took up the opposite wall. Inviting steam rose from the tub.

She stared in amazement. "Wow! This is awesome."

"Compliments can go to my ex-wife. It's her design."

"She has great taste."

"So she told me. In everything except husbands."

"Your bathroom is bigger than the living room of my apartment in Manhattan. Your wife let you keep a house like this after a divorce? What'd she get?"

When he didn't answer, Cheryl glanced at his face. The smiling, teasing cowboy had vanished. It was as if his face had turned to stone.

"She got her freedom," he said at last.

Chapter Three

Sam turned away, but not before Cheryl glimpsed the pain in his eyes. Instantly, she regretted prying into his private life. She knew what it was to carry around things too painful to talk about.

He indicated some clothes on a small wicker stool beside the tub. "I've left you a robe and some sweats you can use when you're done. Call me if you need anything."

He was gone before she could think of a way to apologize. Feeling like a heel, she pulled off her sweater and noticed the bloodstains on her clothes. One more thing

ruined—rental car, job, favorite sweater—
what next? Determined to salvage her clothes,
she hopped to the sink and began filling the
basin with cold water. She glanced into the
mirror and nearly screamed at her gruesome
reflection. With shaky hands, she began to
wash away the blood from her face.

Suddenly, her lip started to tremble as hot
tears stung her eyelids. She dashed them
away with the heels of her hands. She would
not cry. Hopping back to the tub, she tried to
stifle the sobs building inside her. She sat on
the rim and discovered another problem. She
couldn't get her tight-legged pants off over
her swollen ankle. It was the last straw.

Outside Sam had rested his head against
the bathroom door as his anger ebbed away.
Three years, and he still couldn't talk about
Natalie's desertion without feeling a bitterness
that nearly choked him. When she'd left him
with their two small daughters to raise alone,
the hurt had gone bone-deep. The old saying,
Love is blind, was no joke. It had been all too
true for him.

If he ever became involved with another

woman, it'd be with someone who wanted to be a mother to his children. Someone who'd put the twins first, before anything else, and give them the love they deserved. In spite of his surprising attraction to the woman he had rescued tonight, he knew that a New York ballerina didn't fit that bill.

He once let his emotions rule his head and he made a mistake that he was still paying for. But he was wiser now.

He might be wiser, but that didn't stop him from feeling attracted to his visitor. He appreciated Cheryl's sharp wit and quick sense of humor. And he couldn't help but notice that she made a pleasant armful when he held her. He reproached himself for the foolish thought. She was injured, and she needed his help. He turned away from the door, but paused when he heard a noise from inside.

He didn't want to intrude on her privacy, but he wanted to be sure she was okay. He pressed his ear to the door and heard her muffled sobbing. His heart gave a queer little tug at the sound.

She had every right to a good cry. A night

like tonight would have taken the stuffing out of anyone. When she called his name, it surprised him. He took a deep breath, entered the room and stopped short.

She sat on the edge of the tub wrapped in his large robe. Her injured ankle rested on the tub edge with her dark pants bunched around it.

"What's wrong?" he asked.

"I c-can't get m-my pants off o-over my f-foot."

Each hiccuping sob tore at his heart. He watched her struggle to regain control. She didn't like to cry in front of him—he could tell by the way she scrubbed at her tears as they fell. He wanted to offer some comfort but sensed that she would rather recover her composure on her own. He turned to the problem at hand, or rather, at foot.

She was right. Her pant leg wouldn't come off over her swollen ankle. He found a pair of scissors, sat on the tub rim, and began to slit her pant leg up one side.

"The last time I had to do this was when Kayla got a big splinter in her knee. Kayla's one of my daughters. Lindy is her twin. They turned five last October.

"Anyway, Kayla had a long wooden sliver through her jeans. I had to cut them off before I could see how badly she was hurt. Fortunately, it wasn't deep. I thought I was doing fine until I put a bandage on Kayla's knee. Soon as I did, Lindy started wailing."

"Wh-why?"

He glanced at Cheryl and grinned. "She said because she and Kayla weren't ''dentical' anymore. So I had to cut off *her* jeans and put a bandage on her knee too."

Cheryl smiled. "Identical twin girls. I'll bet that's a handful."

"Yes, they are, but I wouldn't have them any other way." He slipped her pants gently over her foot. "There you go."

"Th-thanks for your help."

"Don't mention it. Mom was a teacher, and she taught me to be gallant at all costs."

Startled, Cheryl looked up. Her fingers grew icy-cold, and she pushed them into the deep pockets of his robe as fear tightened the muscles in the back of her neck.

"Does your mother teach near here?" she

asked, trying to sound as if she was making polite conversation and not desperate to know the answer.

"No, she's retired."

Eleanor Hardin had been her junior-high principal. Could Sam be Eleanor's son? How old had her principal been? Cheryl tried to think, but she could only recall the woman with a child's vision. "What about your father?" she asked casually.

"He passed away a few years ago. My grandfather lives here with the twins and I. Nobody knows cattle like Gramps does. You'd never know he was seventy-five. He rides almost every day. Well, I should leave you to finish your bath instead of standing here babbling while the water gets cold." He all but bolted out the door, closing it behind him with a bang.

Relieved at being left alone, Cheryl shed Sam's robe and sank into the whirlpool, leaving her foot with its ice pack propped on the rim. After all the time she'd spent trying to forget the past, why had she ended up so close to it all again?

Was this what Angie had wanted: to see

her big sister exposed and shamed? No, Cheryl didn't believe that. Angie's heart was in the right place, and her intentions were good. Cheryl knew she had only herself to blame. She had chosen the road that led to this disaster.

She kneaded her temples trying to ease the headache pounding away inside her skull. She had to think.

Even if Sam was Eleanor's son, he still had no idea who she was. As long as he continued to think of her as a New York dancer, she'd be safe. And what if he did find out? It wasn't as if she were wanted for a crime. But people out here had long memories and unforgiving natures; she knew that from personal experience. A lot of them would remember that Hank Thatcher's oldest daughter had been in reform school for helping her father steal cattle.

If anyone discovered who she really was, the old story would be out in a flash. Her juvenile records might be sealed, but that wouldn't stop the press from having a field day with the story. No doubt, Grandma Doris would be happy to tell the tale of how her rebellious granddaughter had ended up behind bars. The thought of reliving those painful days made Cheryl feel ill.

It didn't matter what Angie thought, or what Harriet Steele had intended, Cheryl knew she would never go back to the ranch again. It wasn't worth the risk. She had worked too long and too hard to let anything jeopardize the career she loved. She rubbed a weary hand over her face. She had to get away from here.

The soothing hot water began to ease her aches and pains. Slowly she relaxed, and her feeling of panic faded. She was safe for tonight. The storm might keep her here, but it would also keep everyone else away. First thing tomorrow, Sam would drive her to Kansas City, and she could leave the Flint Hills behind forever.

Feeling somewhat better, she finished her bath and washed her hair, being careful of the lump on her temple. After that, she climbed out of the tub and pulled on the gray sweatpants and sweatshirt Sam had left for her. They were big, but comfortable. A search through his medicine cabinet turned up a roll of wide tape, and she expertly wrapped her foot and ankle. It hurt, but she knew it would feel better once she had it taped.

With that done, she washed out her sweater and was pleasantly surprised to find the bloodstains had come out. She hung it to dry on the towel rack and left the room.

Sam came up the stairs in time to see her crossing his living room. Dressed in his old sweats with a towel wrapped turban-style around her head, he could only marvel that anyone could look so graceful and appealing while she hopped on one foot.

He shook his head in resignation. So much for his stern lecture to himself about caring for helpless, injured women. He headed to the bathroom and rummaged in the medicine cabinet until he found a small bottle of pain pills left over from his last run-in with a moody bull.

She was reclining on the sofa when he entered the living room again. Her face looked freshly scrubbed, not a trace of tears anywhere. In his sweats with the sleeves rolled back and a towel around her hair, she looked comfortably at home—as though she belonged here. He dismissed that crazy thought and offered her the pills. "Are you allergic to any medications?"

"Not that I know of. Why?"

"I called the hospital while you were in the tub. They said you could take these if you weren't on any medication or allergic to them."

She took the bottle and read the label. "I've taken these before. They make me sleepy, though."

"That might not be a bad thing. You did a good job wrapping that ankle." The professional-looking bandage impressed him.

"Injuries are a fact of life in my profession. You have to get good at taping joints."

He brought her a glass of water, and she took two of the tablets. "Are you hungry?" he asked.

"A little," she admitted.

"How about a bowl of homemade chicken soup? It'll only take me a minute to heat it up."

She arched one eyebrow. "Don't tell me you know how to make soup from scratch? My image of cowboys may never be the same."

"Good. I haven't had a gun fight in ages,

and I never sing to my horse," he said, heading into the kitchen.

"I'll bet that makes Dusty happy. Anything else I need to know to completely destroy my concept of macho Western men?"

"I can use a vacuum cleaner, and I'm an architect."

"An architect—really?" She glanced around. "Is this one of your designs? It's beautiful."

"Natalie and I collaborated on it."

"Natalie?"

"My ex-wife." For some reason, he suddenly felt the need to explain. "We split up about three years ago. We met in college, two budding architects hot to leave our mark on the world. We seemed to have a lot in common. As it turned out, we didn't. We lived in Kansas City for a while, but after Dad died, I gave up the business and came back to ranch full-time. She didn't care for life out here. She met someone else and that was that."

"I'm sorry. Do you see your children often?"

"The twins live with me, not with their

mother." He looked up with a brittle smile. "She's in China, the last we heard."

"That's a long way from Kansas. What does she do?"

"She's the International Design Director for some big-shot hotel over there."

"Sounds important."

"I'm sure she thinks so."

"Where are your children?" She looked toward the stairs.

"Fortunately for you, they're spending the night with my mother."

Her head snapped around. "Why is that fortunate for me?" she asked, her tone oddly sharp.

Out in the kitchen, Sam laughed. "Let me see if I can enlighten you. 'Why is the sky blue? What holds the clouds up? Why do rocks come in different sizes? Why can't we eat grass like the cows? Why does the sun always come up in the east? Why do we call it *east?*' They never stop talking."

Cheryl smiled, but her mind was racing. How was she going to avoid meeting more of Sam's family? Even if his mother wasn't Eleanor, there had been other Hardins at Jake's and her father's trial. Cheryl was dying to ask specific questions, but she didn't want to arouse Sam's suspicions.

"They sound charming. Do you think they'll be back before I leave?"

"No. Believe me, you do not want to ride in a car with them all the way to Kansas City."

"And your grandfather, will he be joining us? I'm not exactly dressed for company."

"Gramps was asleep when I looked in." Sam carried in two steaming bowls of soup and two glasses of milk on a tray and set it on the coffee table beside her. "I'll pick the girls up on my way back from Kansas City. What about you? Do you have a husband, children?"

Cheryl relaxed once she realized she wasn't going to meet more of his family. "No, no ball and chain or rug rats for me. I can't even take care of a parakeet." She took a bowl of soup from the tray.

Looking up, she realized he wasn't amused by her flippant remark. She had made it sound as though she didn't like children.

"My work comes first," she explained. "I don't have room in my life for anything but dancing. Ballerinas don't usually have long careers. A husband and children will have to wait. Besides, while I was in school I earned money by working at a day-care center. That was enough kid-time to last me for several more years."

"What about other family?" he asked.

Briefly, she considered how to answer. When in doubt, tell the truth—just not all of it. "There's only my sister. I have a half brother somewhere, but we've never kept in touch. My parents are both dead."

A *half brother somewhere* was partly true. As far as she knew, Jake was still in prison. Harriet had kept in touch with him, but she was gone now.

"I always wanted a brother but all I got was a little sister. Becky lives in Denver. I don't get to see her as much as I would like."

To change the subject, Cheryl said, "This is good soup, cowboy."

"Thanks, but you don't have to sound so surprised."

There was a lot about the man that was surprising. She only hoped that his good cooking was the last shock in store for her tonight.

They ate in companionable silence and listened to the sound of the storm outside as the driving snow hissed softly against the tall windows. When she finished, he gathered up her tray and carried it into the kitchen. She tried to hide a yawn, but he saw it.

Walking back to the sofa, he held out his hand. "Come on, New York, it's time you went to bed. You can barely keep your eyes open."

"I thought I would sleep here." She patted the sofa and looked away, uncomfortable with his intense scrutiny.

"Take my bed. You'll be more comfortable, and the bathroom is only a hop away. The guest room is on the lower level, and I don't think you should tackle the stairs. I'll sleep down there."

He made sense, and it wasn't as if she were throwing him out of his bed to sleep on the floor or something. Another yawn convinced her she'd probably fall asleep standing on one foot when the pain pills really kicked in.

"Okay, but I can get there by myself."

"At least lean on me so you don't fall."

She hung on to his arm as they made their way to his bedroom. At the edge of the bed, she sat down just as a yowling, hissing ball of fur erupted from underneath it and attacked her good foot. Cheryl shrieked in surprise and jerked her legs up on the bed.

Sam reached down and scooped up the snarling fury. "Hey, is that any way to treat a guest? Behave yourself. Cheryl, I'd like you to meet Bonkers."

Draped over Sam's arm, the fat, yellow feline turned to stare at her. He wore a smirk remarkably like the Cheshire Cat mask one of her fellow dancers wore in the ballet.

"We call him Bonkers," Sam explained, "because normally he's very sedate, but every once in a while—"

"He just goes bonkers," Cheryl finished. "I get it." She studied the man who held the cat and said, "This tendency runs in the family?"

His grin widened. "Occasionally."

Cheryl massaged her foot. "I was down to only one good foot and now that's full of claw marks."

Sam turned instantly contrite. "Did he hurt you? Bonkers is usually careful not to break the skin. Let me take a look."

"No. I'm fine." She pointed toward the door. "Take the menace and leave."

With a brief salute, Sam did as he was told, taking the cat with him. Cheryl watched the door close, then flopped back and stared at the ceiling fan over the bed.

What was it about Sam Hardin that she found so attractive? They'd met under dramatic circumstances, that could be part of it. She admitted he was good-looking in a rugged sort of way. He was also kind and funny, but it was something more than that. Something she couldn't put her finger on, something she didn't want to examine too closely.

In the end, she decided it was a combination of too much excitement and the strong pain pills. Knowing that she would feel more like her old, sensible self in the morning, she crawled under the thick quilt and settled in. For a while, the painful throbbing in her foot kept sleep at bay, but soon the pain pills did their work, and she drifted off.

Sam fed the cat and retreated to the guest room downstairs. As he lay in the unfamiliar bed, sleep eluded him, and he spent a long time staring at the ceiling. She was sleeping above him.

He berated himself for acting like a fool,

but it didn't help. The woman was dangerous to his peace of mind. Why did she have to be the first one to interest him since Natalie? Why did it have to be a woman who belonged somewhere else?

Come on, Sam, you're thirty-three years old. You're not some kid. You've been there— done that. You don't need her kind of trouble no matter how attractive she is.

He punched his pillow into shape for the tenth time. This was nothing more than the excitement of the night. After all, it wasn't as if he made a habit of rescuing beautiful, intriguing women. Tomorrow he'd drive her to Kansas City and deposit her with her dancing friends, and that would be the end of it.

The sound of the wind finally lulled him to sleep, but Cheryl's face played in and out of his dreams leaving him feeling restless. In the morning, he woke feeling anything but refreshed. He climbed out of bed, dressed and went out to work off his sour mood with chores and shoveling snow.

An incessant ringing woke Cheryl from her drug-induced sleep. She fumbled for the phone on her bedside stand without opening her eyes.

"Hello?" she mumbled into the receiver with her face still pressed into the pillow.

Silence answered her. She tried again a little louder. "Hello?"

"Is Sam there?" a sharp, feminine voice asked.

"Ah—Sam who?" Cheryl muttered, wishing she could just go back to sleep.

"Samuel Hardin. My son."

Cheryl's eyes snapped open. Quickly, she took in the unfamiliar room. In a flash, memory returned.

"Let me speak to Samuel. This is his mother, Eleanor Hardin," the demanding voice hammered in Cheryl's ear.

It *was* her! Cheryl sat up with her heart lodged in her throat.

Chapter Four

Cheryl ran a hand through her tangled hair and winced when she hit the bump on her temple. Sam's mother *was* Eleanor Hardin—former principal of Herington Junior High—and one person who was sure to recognize Cheryl Steele as Cheryl Thatcher.

"You must have the wrong number." Cheryl tried to stay calm.

"Really?" came the unamused reply. "It's rather hard to misdial a number on speed dial, don't you think?"

"Oh, you mean Sam. I'm sorry. I'm still a bit groggy from the drugs he gave me."

"Drugs?" His mother's voice shot up an octave.

"Oh—not those kind of drugs."

"Exactly where is my son?"

"I'm not sure. He said something about staying in the guest room."

"I'm relieved to hear that, at least. Have him call me right away. I don't believe I caught your name."

Cheryl relaxed a tiny bit. Thanks to her acquired New York accent or plain good luck, Sam's mother hadn't recognized her voice.

"It's Cheri," she replied cautiously. It wasn't actually a lie. Some of her friends called her that.

"Thank you, Cheri. Have Sam call me."

The line went dead in Cheryl's hand. She stared at the phone stupidly for a second, then hung up.

Things were rapidly moving from bad to worse. Cheryl had spent too many hours facing Eleanor Hardin across the principal's desk at school for the woman not to recognize her. Those memories were painful to recall, but not as painful as the memory of Mrs. Hardin's testimony before the judge at

Cheryl's juvenile hearing. Eleanor had read Cheryl's own words to the judge. Words from a diary that detailed a troubled girl's desire to lash out at others and to gloat about the crimes she'd gotten away with. Those words had been enough to send Cheryl to a juvenile detention center for nine months.

If only she hadn't written those things. If only Angie hadn't found the diary and taken it to school. If only the book hadn't ended up in Mrs. Hardin's hands. For Cheryl, having her private thoughts exposed to others had been bad enough, but knowing her words had helped send her father and brother to prison had been almost more than she could bear. She didn't want to relive any part of those times.

Snatching up the phone again, she dialed information for the number of the Highway Patrol. She had to find out if the roads were open. She had to get out of here.

Sam entered the front door feeling pleased with himself. He'd fed the stock, the stalls were mucked out and he'd found an old pair of crutches in the toolshed where he kept the snow shovels. He carried them into the house like a trophy. The aroma of fresh coffee greeted him.

New York was in the kitchen. She'd traded in his sweats for her red sweater and black corduroy pants with one leg slit up to the knee. She looked as if she'd slept better than he had.

She was buttering a piece of toast as the coffeemaker sputtered the last drops of coffee into the pot. He glanced around and realized she'd washed the dishes he'd left piled in the sink and put them away. She delayed meeting his gaze when he walked into the kitchen.

He said, "Thanks for cleaning up. You didn't have to do that."

She kept her eyes down, staring at her toast. "It was the least I could do."

Her voice sounded strained, but he couldn't see her eyes. Was she was all right? "You'll do dishes in exchange for a place to sleep? Marry me, baby, you're my kind of woman," he teased.

She shot him a look of disdain. "They don't make that kind of woman anymore, cowboy."

"A guy can hope, can't he?" All right, she

was upset about something, but what? "Is your foot worse?" he tried.

"Looks bad—feels the same." She set her toast and knife down on the counter. "Your mother called this morning. Early."

"So?" Now he was confused.

She arched an eyebrow. "Do strange women often answer your phone at 7:00 a.m. and tell your mother they're still groggy from the drugs you gave them?"

"You didn't."

"I did. You have some explaining to do. She wants you to call her."

"I'm sorry if she embarrassed you. I'll explain, don't worry. She always calls to check on Gramps before we go out to do morning chores. Oh, I found these for you. They may be too tall. If they are, I can shorten them." He handed her the crutches and started for the stairs

When he came up half an hour later, she saw he wasn't alone. An elderly man with snow-white hair and piercing dark eyes behind thick glasses accompanied him. His slightly stooped frame was clad in blue jeans, a plaid shirt and worn cowboy boots.

She watched the older Hardin's expression intently as Sam introduced them, expecting to be denounced on the spot.

"Pleased to make your acquaintance," Walter Hardin said as he sank down on the sofa beside her. "Sam tells me you're from New York City."

"I am." Her knees went weak as she sensed a reprieve.

"I took a trip to New York once. It was crowded, but folks were a lot nicer than I'd been led to expect."

She smiled, almost giddy with relief. She didn't recognize Walter Hardin and saw little to indicate that he might recognize her. Maybe the trial of her father and brother hadn't attracted as much attention as she imagined. Or maybe it had simply been so long ago that people had forgotten it.

She said, "I called the Highway Patrol this morning. Everything south of I-70 and east of US 77 is closed."

"I figured as much," Walter said. "Hope you don't mind spending a little time with us."

"You and your grandson have been very kind, but I really need to get to Kansas City."

Sam took a seat across from them. "The snow has stopped, but until this wind lets up, the roads will drift shut as fast as the crews can open them. The forecast is calling for warmer temperatures tomorrow. It'll melt fast once that happens."

She finally asked the question that had been burning on the tip of her tongue. "Will your mother be bringing your children home soon?" She had to be gone before Eleanor Hardin showed up.

Sam shook his head. "No, they're snowed in, too. The girls want to stay a few days, and Mom doesn't mind. I'll pick them up after we find a way to get you to Kansas City."

Cheryl relaxed. It seemed a little good luck had finally come her way.

Walter pushed himself up from the sofa. "That coffee smells good. I think I'll fix myself a cup. You want one, Sammy?"

"Sure, Gramps."

As the elder Hardin made his way to the kitchen, Sam turned to Cheryl. "Do the crutches fit you?"

"They're too tall, Sammy. But the autograph is priceless."

"What?"

"They're signed, To Sammy, with all my love, Merci."

He chuckled and took the crutch from her to read the faded writing along the edge. "I'd forgotten about that. She said she didn't want to sign my cast, she wanted to sign my crutches because then her name would be closer to my heart."

"How romantic."

He shook his head. "We were in high school."

"That must have been hard. With your mother as a teacher, I mean."

"Mom taught over in the next school district. Believe me, I think I would have transferred schools before I became one of her pupils. She was strict as they come. I hear they called her Hard-as-Nails Hardin over in Herington."

Cheryl bit her lip to keep from making a comment. The kids at school *had* called her that, and worse. "Tell me about your old flame."

"She's a friend."

"'With all my love?' That's more than friendly, Sammy."

"Okay, we were an item in high school. Now, we're just—good friends."

By his hesitation, Cheryl wondered if the fires of this particular high-school flame weren't entirely dead. "You still see each other?"

"Occasionally. How much shorter do these need to be?"

Cheryl remained curious about the woman who lingered in Sam's affections, but let the subject drop. After he'd adjusted the crutches, she tried them out again. Swinging herself across the room, she said, "This is much better. Thank you." Turning around, she headed toward the front door.

"Where do you think you're going?" he demanded.

"To get my purse. I think I left it out in the entryway last night."

It was still lying on the bench where she had left it, but when she picked it up, she had an unpleasant surprise. It felt too light. A quick check showed her wallet was missing.

She was on her knees looking under the bench when Sam came up behind her.

"What's wrong?" he asked.

"My wallet is gone."

"Are you sure?"

She rolled her eyes and gave him a don't-be-stupid look. "Of course, I'm sure. It must have fallen out of my purse during the accident last night." A sudden thought hit her, and she looked at him sharply. "Unless you have it."

He helped her to her feet. "Why would I take your wallet?" Clearly, he seemed puzzled by her accusation.

To check up on me? To see if I'm really who I claim to be?

Paranoia seemed to be leaking out her pores. If she wasn't careful she would give him a reason to do just that. "I meant, maybe you found it and forgot to give it to me," she finished lamely.

"I haven't seen it," he said.

She gave him a bright smile. "Then it's still in my car."

"In this weather, it'll be safe enough."

"True, but I'd feel better if I had it. My

credit cards, checkbook, driver's license, everything is in it."

"I have to ride out and check on some cows that are due to calve. I'll look for it on my way home. Can I bring back anything else from your car?"

She sat down on the bench. "If you think you could manage my suitcase, that would be great. So you really are a cattle rancher, not simply an architect who lives in the country?"

"Yes, ma'am. You're looking at the breeder of some of the finest Charolais cattle in the Midwest. That's what I was doing out last night. Moving cattle into the barns. Most of the calves have already been born, but I still have a few cows that are due to calve soon. I didn't want the little critters to be born out in a snowdrift."

Cheryl burst out laughing at the image.

"What's so funny?" he demanded.

"That paints such a great picture. You trying to round up white cows and their little white calves in a snowstorm." Her laughter died away when she saw the speculative look on his face. Suddenly, she knew she'd made a mistake.

"How does a girl from New York City know what color Charolais cattle are?"

She raised a hand to her temple to ease the sudden pain in her head. How could she answer? She couldn't lie to him, but she didn't want Sam to know who she really was. Cheryl Steele from New York was talented, self-assured and witty. Cheryl Thatcher had been a sad, pitiful creature. It would be best if she never came back.

The cat chose that moment to leap into her lap. Cheryl jumped, startled by the animal. "Bonkers, you scared me to death. Don't you get tired of attacking people?"

"Hardly ever," Walter supplied as he came in with a steaming mug in each hand. He gave one to Sam.

Cheryl avoided looking at Sam or his grandfather. "I have such a headache this morning. I think I'll go lie down for a while."

"Is there anything we can do?" Walter asked, his concern evident.

"No, thank you." She pushed the cat off her lap and left the room moving slowly on her crutches.

Sam watched her go and realized she hadn't

answered his question. And what had caused the dark pain that filled her eyes so briefly? Maybe it had been her headache, but he had the feeling there was more to it than that. She presented an interesting puzzle. One minute she was smiling and laughing, the next minute she looked like a scared, lost waif.

She's not your puzzle to solve, Sam reminded himself. Don't forget that fact.

After discussing his plans for the day with Gramps, Sam headed downstairs to his office, but he couldn't get his mind off his houseguest. He admitted he was attracted to Cheryl, intrigued by her even, but he wasn't a fool. For his own peace of mind, it would be best to remember she'd be gone soon.

He busied himself in his office for the remainder of the morning and worked on his latest project. He loved designing homes almost as much as he loved ranching, and he'd missed it since he came back to take over the homestead. In spite of his father's and grandfather's experience, years of poor cattle markets, dry weather and bad investments had left the ranch on the verge of ruin.

It'd taken every scrap of Sam's time and most of his money to get the place back on its feet. This year, with the income from his breeding program, he stood to make a real profit for the first time in years. Enough to let the ranch survive.

That time might have come sooner if he hadn't spent so much money building this house. He had used the construction to try to keep Natalie happy. And she had used it to dupe him.

Every trip she'd taken to Kansas City for the best glass, the right tile, the most unique rugs, had only been a cover to meet her boyfriend, and Sam had never suspected anything until it was too late. It had been a bitter lesson to learn.

He turned his attention back to his design. Thanks to his former partner in Kansas City, he now had the chance to work for the firm again. The added income would provide a much-needed cushion for the ranch. A lot hinged on the home he was designing here. If all went well, construction would begin on the massive stone house on a hillside outside of Kansas City within the month. The only drawback was that it meant he'd need to travel to Kansas City frequently over the next few weeks.

A little after one o'clock, he put his plans away and headed upstairs. There was no sign of Cheryl, so he fixed a tray of toasted cheese sandwiches and a salad, then knocked on her door.

"Come in," her groggy voice called.

He opened the door and carried the tray inside. "I thought you might like some lunch."

"Um, sounds great." She raised up on one elbow and pushed her hair out of her face. "What time is it?"

"One-thirty. The wind's died down, and I'm going to ride over and check the cattle. I wanted to let you know I was leaving."

"Be careful out there." Worry tinged her voice and put a small frown line between her beautiful blue eyes.

"I will. Besides, Dusty always comes straight home after work."

"Make sure you're on him."

She looked adorable with her hair mussed and her eyes still cloudy with sleep. He deposited the tray and quickly turned to leave. Bonkers made a dash inside as Sam started to close the door. The cat jumped on the bed and began to butt his head against her side for attention.

She ran a hand down his back and he purred loudly. "I think your cat is beginning to like me."

"I think you're beginning to like my cat."

"He's persistent. I admire that." She picked Bonkers up and rubbed a knuckle under his chin. A look of bliss crossed the big cat's face.

Sam turned and stomped out of the room feeling ridiculous. He couldn't be jealous of a cat. What he needed was a long, cold ride in the snow to take his mind off his very charming visitor.

Hours later, Cheryl sat in Sam's living room waiting with his grandfather. Both of them anxiously watched the clock. Sam had been gone far longer than he should have been. It was almost dark. At the sound of the door opening, she and Walter hurried out to the entryway. Sam paused inside the doorway and set her suitcase down. He looked cold, tired and worried.

"Is everything okay?" she asked.

"I've got some bad news, New York."

"Did we lose some calves?" Walter asked.

She crossed her arms over her chest and shivered in the cold draft. She knew the loss of even a few head could spell financial disaster for some ranchers. How many ranchers had been put in financial jeopardy by her family? She hated to think about it.

"The cattle are all okay, but your wallet wasn't in the car, Cheryl."

"What? Are you sure?"

"I'm sure."

Walter said, "You look terrible, Son. Cheryl made hot cocoa earlier. Would you like some? I could make coffee if you'd rather."

"Cocoa sounds great."

Cheryl hobbled to the kitchen with them. Sam shed his coat with a weary sigh. Walter filled a thick, white mug with the steaming drink and held it out to Sam. He took the cup and sipped it. "Man, this hits the spot."

He sank into a chair at the table. "I searched all through your car. There weren't any tracks in the snow, so no one else had been in it since the snow stopped. Is it possible it fell out on the ride back?"

"I guess it's possible—my purse was unzipped. Did you look around the outside of the car?"

"I tried, but there's too much snow yet. Hey, we know we only rode along the highway and down my lane, so it's out there somewhere. We'll find it when the snow melts."

"When the snow melts! When might that be?" Cheryl snapped. She couldn't wait for the snow to melt. The longer she stayed, the more likely it was that Sam would find out who she really was. The daughter of a felon, one of those "thieving Thatchers," as people in the community had labeled her family. Someone who had spent time in reform school instead of prison only because of her age.

It wasn't fair. She wasn't that person anymore. She was the "Steel Ballerina," the darling of New York's young ballet set. How would her fans or the press react when they heard she had been convicted of cattle rustling and assaulting a sheriff's deputy? At best, she'd become a laughingstock. At worst, her career would suffer. All because she'd taken this stupid side trip.

"I can't believe my rotten luck!" She shuffled to the far side of the room, narrowly missing the cat's tail with her crutches when she swung around. Bonkers scrambled out of her way.

"Take it easy," Sam cautioned. "You're making me feel like I should take cover with the cat."

"This is serious, Sam!"

"I know, but don't worry. We'll find it. Have a little faith."

"Don't worry? I need my driver's license, my money and my credit cards. I need to catch up with my company before they leave Kansas City. If I'm not dancing by then, I'm out of a job for the entire spring. Don't worry? I can't even go back to New York. I sublet my apartment until the end of June because I was going to be on this tour."

She was tired, her foot ached like a bad tooth and all he could say was, "Don't worry."

"What about your sister? Can you stay with her?"

"Yesterday was my sister's wedding,

remember? She's on her honeymoon in Hawaii. I doubt the happy couple booked an extra room for me."

"Okay, calm down. Things will work out, you'll see. The snow can't last more than a few days."

"Oh, that's just like a man. Calm down and wait till the snow melts! I can't believe this! Nothing has gone right since I set foot in this stupid state!" She hobbled out of the room slamming the bedroom door behind her.

Walter stared after her. "There's something about that gal that seems familiar."

"She has a temper like Natalie's. That's what makes her seem familiar. Women like her don't have any understanding or patience for the forces of nature. They want the world to jump for them when they snap their fingers."

"You're wrong to judge all women using Natalie as a yardstick, Sam."

"I know, but I can't help it. Once burned— twice shy." What he didn't admit was how attracted he was to Cheryl and how it scared him. He knew she was a woman every bit as wrong for him as his ex-wife had been.

Chapter Five

Cheryl opened the bedroom door early the next morning and peeked out. There was no sign of Sam or Walter. Bonkers came to weave around her legs and meow at her. She picked him up and rubbed her chin on his head. The blinds on the glass wall were open. Now that the driving snow had stopped, early-morning sunshine poured through the tall windows. She put the cat down and crossed the room on her crutches to take a closer look at the spectacular view spread before her.

Sam's home sat on the very edge of a steep bluff. The balcony that ran the full length of the house outside the windows gave the illusion of a house suspended in midair. In the valley below, frosted trees outlined the winding course of a small creek. Beyond them the prairie rose again to flat-topped, snow-covered bluffs and sparkling rounded hills that rolled away as far as she could see. Overhead, the brilliant blue sky arched like an azure bowl over a dazzling, glittering world. Her mother would have loved this view.

Cheryl laid her forehead against the cool window glass. Her mother had loved every rock and blade of these vast grasslands. Even after her friends and neighbors had turned against her. Cheryl had never understood it. And she'd never understood why her gentle mother had stayed with Hank Thatcher.

A womanizer, a bully and a drunk, her father was always angry. Her earliest memory was of hiding behind the sofa and listening to the sounds of her mother weeping. The only happy times in her childhood had been when her father wasn't home.

Mira Thatcher had been Hank's second wife. As she grew older, Cheryl suspected that her mother stayed because of Hank's son.

Jake, Cheryl's half brother, was eight years her senior, and Mira loved him like one of her own.

Cheryl was nine the first time her father and Jake were arrested and convicted of stealing cattle. The condemnation of the ranching community, the pitying looks, the whispers behind their backs made life hard for Mira and her daughters, but at least Hank had been out of the picture. When Cheryl turned eleven, her father and brother came home, but things only got worse. That summer, her mother died.

Drunk as usual, Cheryl's father had been driving when the accident happened, yet he survived with barely a scratch. The day after her mother's funeral, Grandma Doris moved in with them. That year was the worst year of Cheryl's life.

A hard and bitter woman, Doris Thatcher wielded her strict discipline with a heavy hand. No one was exempt from the sharp edge of her tongue. She harped endlessly at her son to stop drinking, straighten up, get some work done—the list went on and on. Hank ignored her, and Jake had simply moved out, leaving Cheryl and Angie to bear the brunt of her harsh lessons punctuated with blows from a leather strap.

At school, Cheryl had been equally miserable, but she hid her feelings behind a wall of anger. Protective of Angie and sensitive about her family, she made an easy target for the taunts of the other kids. She never backed away from a fight—even the ones she knew she couldn't win. For that reason, she often wound up in the principal's office facing Eleanor Hardin.

Eleanor had been one of Mira Thatcher's few friends. Maybe that was why her disappointment in Cheryl's behavior had been so blatantly obvious. In the face of it all, Cheryl had remained stubbornly silent about her treatment at home. When pressed, she resorted to belligerence, and that attitude made it easy for people to believe the worst of her later. "Like father, like daughter," they said. After a while, Cheryl stopped caring about what they thought.

But it had all happened so long ago.

Cheryl turned away from the window. She had changed more than her name since then;

she had changed who she was inside. At least, she had believed that until she found herself back in Kansas.

She worried her lower lip between her teeth. From the time she had driven away from her grandmother's ranch, Cheryl had found herself hiding from and skirting around the truth the way she had done as a child.

Determined not to dwell on the uncomfortable thought, she donned her leotard and spent the next hour performing the exercises and stretches that kept her body flexible and graceful for the dance. It was hard work, awkward and painful with her swollen foot, but she welcomed the pain as a distraction from her unsettling thoughts.

Finally, when she finished her morning routine, she flopped down on the sofa and put her aching foot up on a pillow. A moment later she heard the front door open. She looked up and a tingle of anticipation fluttered in the pit of her stomach.

Sam entered the living room and stopped short when he caught sight of Cheryl lying on his sofa. Her hair was pulled back into a ponytail, but a few wisps had escaped and the sweat-dampened curls clung to her sculptured cheeks and the slender column of her neck. She wore a black leotard, pink, calf-length yoga pants and only one shoe with white ribbons that crisscrossed her delicate ankle. Her other foot lay propped on a pillow, and he saw the blue-black bruising and swelling extending above and below the edges of the tape she had wrapped it with.

"You shouldn't be using that foot." His admonishment came out sounding gruffer than he intended.

Clearly miffed at his scolding, her lips pressed into a tight line. Would they soften if he kissed her? Where had that thought come from?

"I know what I'm doing," she said.

He was saved from making a reply by the ringing of the phone. As he answered it, Cheryl picked up her crutches and went to busy herself in the kitchen until he joined her a short while later.

Glancing up from her coffee mug, she saw the worried look on his face. "What's the matter?"

"That was my mother. My sister was taken to the hospital last night."

"Oh, Sam, I'm so sorry. Is it serious?"

"Becky is pregnant, but she's not due for another ten weeks. She started into early labor. The doctors were able to stop it, but she has to stay on strict bed rest."

"Can you get to the hospital? Are the roads open?"

"Becky and Michael live in Colorado."

"I see." Cheryl poured him a cup of coffee. "Is it her first baby?"

"No, they have three. That's part of the reason Mom called. She'll be on her way to Denver as soon as the roads are open to help Michael take care of the kids." He sipped the coffee she'd given him.

"Three kids would be a handful for a man with his wife in the hospital."

"Yeah, well, two kids will be a handful for me with the ranch work and a house going up in Kansas City. Mom takes care of the twins while I'm working."

"What will you do?" she asked in concern.

"I guess I'll have to start looking for a temporary nanny. I hope, for Becky's sake as well as my own, that she gets out of the hospital soon." He lifted his mug in a small salute. "You make a good cup of coffee, New York."

"Thanks, cowboy." She stared into the dark liquid of her own cup. "Sam, I want to apologize for taking my foul temper out on you last night. You've been more than kind to me, and I'm sorry I repaid you by acting like a spoiled child."

"Apology accepted. And as much as I like that outfit, I think you should change into something warmer."

She frowned at him. "Why?"

"The snow's melting fast. I think I can get you into Council Grove and have a doctor look at that foot."

Cheryl bit her lip in indecision. She needed to see a doctor—she suspected there was more wrong with her foot than a sprain—but could she risk running into someone in Council Grove who might recognize her?

"Can't you get me to Manhattan or Kansas City?" she asked hopefully. "I could see a doctor there."

He shook his head. "Sorry. They had more

snow north of here. The roads aren't open in that direction yet."

"I hate to put you to more trouble, Sam. I'll be fine for another day."

"No, you won't. You need to get that foot looked at. I'm taking you and that's final."

She couldn't think of a good reason to argue with him.

Thirty minutes later, they were bumping along the lane and out onto the highway. The ride was rough, but Sam handled the truck with a skill she had to admire. They arrived in Council Grove a little battered but none the worse for the trip.

She reluctantly agreed to let Sam cover the cost of the E.R. visit until she found her wallet and could send the hospital a copy of her insurance card. It was not an arrangement she liked, but she couldn't see any alternative.

Through her wide, round sunglasses, she studied the occupants of the small hospital's waiting room as she waited for her turn to see the doctor, noting thankfully that none of the faces looked familiar. Cowboys, farmers and housewives discussed cattle, crop losses and sick kids. The weather dominated the conversations going on around her. Nothing had changed much in the years she'd been gone.

She studied the worn linoleum on the floor and tried to decide what she would do if her foot were broken. She reviewed the list of friends she could stay with until her apartment was available again, but it was a pretty short list. Even getting back to New York would be difficult without money or credit cards. Her sister would be home in a few weeks. Cheryl didn't want to impose on the newlyweds, but her savings wouldn't pay the bills and the cost of a motel for a month or more. All in all, things looked pretty bleak.

"Why, Sam! What are you doing here? You're not sick, I hope? Is something wrong with the girls?"

Cheryl looked up to see a tall redhead eyeing Sam as if he were a free lunch and she hadn't had a bite all week. The woman sauntered across the room and stopped in front of him, but her gaze pinned Cheryl like a hawk.

Cheryl knew the look—she'd been subjected to it more than once. She was being assessed as a potential rival. The redhead definitely had her sights set on Sam.

"The girls are fine," Sam said. "I'm here with a friend. You're looking well, Merci. How's the new job going?"

"Good, thanks. We're busier today than usual." The woman turned her gaze on Cheryl. "I don't believe we've met. I'm Merci Slader. I'm a unit clerk here at the hospital."

So this was Merci, Sam's old flame. "Cheryl Steele," she offered her hand.

Merci took it in a limp grip. Her smile was definitely frosty. "I don't recall Sam mentioning you before."

"We've only just met. I'm sure he'll have a lot to say about me later. Won't you, cowboy?" Cheryl patted his knee.

"What happened to your leg, dear? Did you trip and fall?" Merci's voice was more than a little catty.

Cheryl laughed, "No, I had a car accident in the storm. Fortunately, Sam came along in time to rescue me, and we got—stuck together!"

"Miss Steele, the doctor can see you now,"

a plump gray-haired nurse called from the doorway.

Cheryl rose gracefully and leaned on her crutches. "It was so nice talking to you. Do keep Sam company while the doctor looks at my foot, won't you? I know how he likes to visit with *old* friends." She cast Sam an innocent smile and swung across the room.

Half an hour later, Cheryl had lost her cheeky attitude. She sat on the exam table while Dr. Carlton pointed out the two fractured bones that put an end to her income and plans for the entire spring.

"I've spoken to your physician in New York. He has made a few recommendations, but I'm not sure I can carry them out." The middle-aged doctor was a comical figure, short, bald and rotund, but he spoke with professional politeness.

Cheryl chewed her lip a moment. "What did Dr. Fuller have to say?"

"He recommended I put you in an extra-heavy cast, then add a ball and chain to see if that'd slow you down." He peered at her from over the edge of his reading glasses. "Seems he's had a mite of trouble keeping you off an injury in the past."

Cheryl had the grace to look shamefaced.

"I see evidence of an old fracture here, but it's healed well." He pointed it out on the black-and-white X-ray film as he held it up to the light.

"Isn't there something else we can do besides cast it, Dr. Carlton? I've got to be able to work again soon."

He lowered the film and faced her. "I think you know the answer to that. Do you want to continue to dance?"

"More than I want to breathe."

"I believe that. Now, if you want to dance the way Dr. Fuller tells me you can, you will let me set these bones, cast your foot and you'll keep off it for six to eight weeks."

"But—"

"No, don't interrupt me, young lady. You have had a crushing injury. Your tendons and muscles, as well as your bones, need time to heal. Your other choice is surgery to pin the bones. I'd send you back to Dr. Fuller for that, but you would still be off that foot for at least six weeks."

"Those are my choices?"

"If you want this foot to heal well enough to continue your career, yes."

She nodded in resignation.

"Good. By the way, Dr. Fuller is having his office fax over your insurance information. At least that will be one less worry for you." He stood and opened the door of the small room, then paused. "Have we met before? You look familiar somehow."

She glanced up in surprise. Why would he think that? She was sure she'd never met him. Her infrequent visits to the doctor as a child had been to an elderly physician in the neighboring town of Herington more than thirty miles away.

"No, I don't believe we have," she said. "Unless you've been to New York lately."

He shook his head. "It'll come to me. I never forget a face. I'll have the nurse give you a sedative before I set that foot. I'm afraid this won't be fun."

Dr. Carlton was a master at understatements. It was not fun.

An hour later, Sam half carried her to his

truck and settled her with care on the seat. "Are you all right?"

"Everything's spinning like a top. My foot's throbbing like a wild thing. This cast weighs a ton, and whatever medicine they gave me is making me sick. Other than that, cowboy, I'm peachy."

She sat up straight, determined to prove she was all right. She noticed Merci Slader watching them from the front of the hospital. The woman didn't look happy. Merci shouldn't worry. Cheryl had no designs on Sam.

Someone else was watching them. Cheryl could just make out a face in the frost-covered window beside the door. There was something familiar about it. A chill ran up her spine.

"Are you ready to go?"

Sam was beside her waiting to close the truck door. She glanced at him, then back to the hospital. The face in the window was gone.

Had she imagined it? The painkillers the doctor had given her were certainly making her feel weird. She closed her eyes, leaned her head back. "I'm ready. I think."

Sam kept a close eye on her as they bounced along the highway through deep tire ruts in the snow. He could see she was in pain, but she wasn't one to complain.

"Sam, stop the truck," she insisted suddenly.

"What for?"

"Stop now!"

He stepped on the brake and the pickup slid to an abrupt halt. She opened the door, stepped out and was thoroughly sick at the side of the road.

Sam hurried around the truck, dropped to one knee at her side, and held her as she retched. Carefully, he gathered her hair back and held it away from her face. It felt like soft strands of the finest silk as it curled around his hand.

What was there about this woman that got under his skin so easily? She could talk and act like the most independent woman in the world, but he couldn't shake the feeling she needed someone to take care of her. Someone like him.

He marveled at his own foolishness. He was in deep trouble if holding a woman while she was being sick struck him as romantic. The realization that she would be gone from his life in a day or two brought a sharp twist of regret.

He continued to hold her, talking soothing nonsense until her spasms passed. After a few minutes he was able to get her back in the truck, but she was shaking like a leaf, and her face was pasty pale.

"I'm sorry," she moaned.

Sam wet his bandanna in the melting snow and used it to wipe her face. Her eyes flew open at the touch of the cold cloth. She gave him a limp little half smile, but it didn't ease his mind.

"Do I need to take you back to the hospital?" he asked.

"No, I'll live. That cold cloth feels wonderful. I've always wondered why cowboys wore bandannas, now I know. They're great for first aid."

Her voice sounded so forlorn Sam couldn't help himself. He leaned in and kissed her forehead. "You women gave up wearing petticoats, so someone had to carry the bandages. Are you ready to go?"

She nodded, leaned her head back and closed her eyes. She was asleep before Sam got around to the driver's seat. He shifted her until she was lying along the seat with her head on his leg. He sat for a moment and let his fingers linger on her cheek. Yes, he would be sorry to see her go. He put the truck in gear and drove slowly home.

At the ranch, she stirred as he lifted her out of the pickup, but she didn't wake. He carried her into the house and laid her gently on his bed, then he stood back and watched her as she slept. She was a tough little character. He reached down to smooth a lock of hair from her face, and she smiled in her sleep at his touch.

He liked her, Sam realized. He liked this tough, sassy, graceful-as-a-willow young woman. She stirred him in so many ways. She was beautiful, true, but her quick mind drew him more than her pretty face. She made him laugh, but at the same time she made him feel strong and protective. He tried to be objective about his feelings toward her, but she gave a soft snore, and it chased his objectivity away. He smiled but it was touched with sadness. She wasn't for him.

She wouldn't stay, he knew that even as he found himself wishing for a way to keep her here longer. He wanted time to sort out his feelings. To see if this was an infatuation or something deeper. He'd tried to harden his heart against her, but in spite of his best efforts, she'd hobbled right into the one spot that had been lonely and empty too long.

Why was she here? To test him, or to heal him? He might never learn the answer. He simply had to have faith that there was a reason. He closed the bedroom door and headed for his office.

Bonkers lay stretched out along the back of the sofa in his favorite spot, but suddenly, he jumped up and took off for the front door. An explosion of sound came from the entryway. Squeals, giggles and the sound of running feet.

A pair of identical five-year-old girls flew into the room and wrapped themselves around Sam's legs.

"Did you—" one girl began.

"—miss us?" the other finished.

Sam shook his head. "Nope."

"Yes, you did."

"You missed us."

Sam looked up to see his mother smiling indulgently from the doorway. "Okay, maybe a little."

"We had lots of fun at Grandma's," Lindy said, clearly excited by her time away from home.

"Can we go outside and play now?" Kayla asked.

"Can we get—" Lindy began.

"—our sled out?" Kayla finished her sister's sentence as the twins often did, much to the bemusement of those who knew them.

Sam lifted them up, one in each arm, and looked into the two most important faces in his life. "Kisses first," he said. Two sturdy sets of arms circled his neck, and smacking kisses covered his cheeks. His heart expanded in his chest until he thought it might burst.

Eleanor Hardin walked in and began pulling off her gloves. "If I had known they were going to be snowed in with me, I would have been busy when you called and asked me to watch them."

He smiled and shook his head. "No, you wouldn't have. You loved every minute of it. Come in."

"I can't stay. I've got to get on the road."

"You're driving to Denver now? Is I-70 open already?"

"Yes, to both questions."

He could see her searching the room with her eyes. "Cheryl is resting right now," he said. "The doctor set her broken foot this morning, and she's sleeping off the sedation."

Eleanor looked perplexed. "I thought her name was Cheri."

"Who's Cheri?" the twins asked simultaneously.

"It's Cheryl," Sam answered.

"Her foot really is broken? The poor dear." A slender woman with a short gray bob, Eleanor was dressed in jeans and a bulky green sweater. She swooped in and took charge as usual.

She plucked the girls out of his arms and set them down. "Go change into your snowsuits.

Daddy will take you outside, but not until you're dressed, including mittens."

"Who's Cheryl?" the twins insisted, jumping up and down.

"Girls, listen," Sam said sternly. "Cheryl is our guest and she's sleeping in my room, so you'll have to be quiet."

An identical mulish look appeared on their faces so he knelt in front of them. "You can't wake her up. Understand?"

"Yes, Daddy," they replied together.

"Good. Now, go get dressed for sledding while I walk Grandma out to the car."

The twins took off for the stairs. Picking up Bonkers, Kayla said, "You can ride—"

"—on the sled, too," Lindy told the cat.

Eleanor turned back to Sam. "Bonkers doesn't look thrilled, does he? Son, I'm sorry to leave you in such a fix."

He could see she was genuinely torn about leaving. He draped his arm over her shoulder and gave her a squeeze. "Now, Mom, Becky needs you. Tell her the girls and I will keep her in our thoughts. Go. Don't worry about us. We'll be okay."

She reached up and pulled his head down to

give him a quick peck on the cheek. "I know you will—you always are. I wish I could meet your Cheri."

"Cheryl, Mom, and she isn't mine. I told you, she's a ballet dancer touring the country with her company. She's been stranded here for a couple of days by the storm, that's all. If I-70's open, she'll be able to get to Kansas City tomorrow and rejoin her friends."

"If her foot is broken, she certainly can't dance."

"I know. I've been thinking about that. Maybe she could stay and help take care of the girls until you get back? If she can't work, she might be happy to take the job."

"Are you certain you want to ask a stranger to watch the girls, Sam? That isn't like you. What do you know about her?"

Not as much as he would like to know, he realized. "It was just an idea."

"I'm not sure someone on crutches would be able to keep up with your two little whirlwinds."

"The girls can entertain themselves. Even with her leg in a cast, she should be able to manage them with Gramps to help."

"I know I'm leaving you in a lurch, but please think this over carefully."

"I will. You know me, I never do anything without a lot of thought."

"True. Now, walk me out to my car. There are some things I'll need you to take care of while I'm gone. I have a small list of things for you to do."

"Small? Knowing you, it's as long as my leg."

"Nonsense. It's only as long as your arm."

With a laugh, Sam followed his mother out the door.

At the stairwell, two little girls stuck their heads up and checked to see if the coast was clear, then they crossed to their father's bedroom still lugging the enormous cat.

Chapter Six

Cheryl woke to a nagging ache in her foot and trouble breathing. It felt like a twenty-pound weight pressing down on her chest. She opened her eyes and found herself staring into the cat's broad face. A yellow twenty-pound, fur-covered weight.

"Bonkers, get off." She gave him a not-so-gentle shove.

She was in Sam's room again, she realized, yet she couldn't remember how she'd gotten here. A slight noise caught her attention, and she turned her head.

Two identical little girls peered at her over

the edge of the mattress. Their chins were propped on chubby hands and their elbows rested on the bed. The cat sat between them watching her with an unblinking stare.

Cheryl closed her eyes. "Let me guess. Tweedledee and Tweedledum?"

She opened one eye slowly. The pair remained. They watched her with solemn brown eyes, much darker than their father's, but their short chestnut hair held a multitude of curls like his. It seemed she was going to meet Sam's children, after all.

"Hi." Cheryl spoke slowly—her mouth felt as if it had been stuffed with cotton. "You must be Lindy and Kayla."

They nodded.

"I'm Cheryl." Coming fully awake, she sat up and cast a fearful glance toward the door. "Is your grandmother here?"

"She went to see—" the one on the right started.

"—Aunt Becky in Denver," the one on the left finished.

Light-headed with relief, Cheryl leaned back on her elbows. Her luck had held.

The Queen of Hearts wasn't going to come running in and demand her head.

Cheryl eyed the bulky white cast on her leg. Her foot was broken, she was out of a job and she had no place to live. Some luck.

"Did Bonkers—" began the one on the right.

"—wake you up?" finished the one on the left.

Cheryl smiled to reassure them. "He did, but that's okay."

The twins looked at each other silently for a long moment. Cheryl detected a twinkle, very much like their father's, sparkling in the depths of their brown eyes. Bonkers lifted a paw and gave it a lick.

"Daddy said—"

"—we can't wake you up, but—"

"—he didn't say, Bonkers—"

"—couldn't wake you up."

Cheryl followed the twisted logic, but she was having trouble following the single conversation coming from the two children. She scooted up in bed and leaned against the headboard, gritting her teeth as a stab of pain shot up her leg. "Do you always do that?"

"Do what?" they asked together.

"Finish each other's sentences."

Again, that look flashed between them. "Not always," they replied together again.

"I know your names are Lindy and Kayla, but which one is which?"

"You have to guess."

"How'd you hurt your foot?"

"How'd the doctor get that cast on?"

"Can you still—"

"—wiggle your toes?"

Cheryl smiled. "I think your father tried to warn me about you and your questions."

"Daddy likes you," remarked the child on the right.

"Yes, he does," the girl on the left added. She picked up the cat, draped him over her shoulder, and they all trooped out of the room. Cheryl eyed the bedroom door for a while, but the Mad Hatter and the White Rabbit didn't show.

She left the bed an hour later still feeling unsteady, but she managed the crutches well enough. The pain in her foot was bearable if she didn't move too fast or bump it. There was no one in the kitchen or the living room, and Cheryl toyed with the idea of going back to bed until she heard the sound of shouting outside.

She crossed to the sliding glass door that led to the balcony and eased it open. A crisp, cold breeze blew in, lifting the ends of her hair and chasing the last of the cobwebs from her mind as it carried the sound of children's laughter to her.

Leaning a shoulder against the door frame, Cheryl watched the sledding party in progress on the slope of the opposite hillside. Sam stood behind the twins as they piled on a red sled. He steadied it, then gave a shove that sent them squealing and shrieking to the bottom of the hill. They tumbled out of the sled, trudged back to the top and started all over again.

Cheryl smiled with amusement as Bonkers crept up to investigate the sled. The twins picked him up and settled him in between them. Sam gave them a push, and they flew down the hill again. Halfway down, Bonkers apparently decided he didn't care for the ride. He jumped out but went rolling and sliding down the snowy slope. The twins shrieked in alarm as they hurried toward the snow-covered cat.

Bonkers didn't wait for help. He picked himself up with wounded dignity and stalked off, shaking his paws with every other step. Cheryl laughed aloud at the cat's antics. She saw Sam laughing, too.

He must have heard her because he looked up and gave her a brief wave. She waved back. A warm glow settled in the center of her chest as she watched him playing with his children. This was a new side of him. It couldn't be easy raising two small daughters, but he seemed up to the job. He was certainly enjoying himself now. He even took a turn on the sled as the girls shouted encouragement.

Cheryl covered her smile with one hand. What a comical figure he made when he sat on the small sled. His long legs were bent with his knees drawn up almost to his ears. With one hand, he kept his hat jammed on his head. The other hand he held high in the air like a bronc rider as the twins pushed him off the hilltop. His grin was as big as all outdoors, and Cheryl had no trouble imagining the boy he'd once been as he flew down the hill and tipped over at the bottom.

An unexpected stab of jealousy pierced her as she watched Sam and his girls. Her father had never played with her and her sister; he had never smiled and laughed with them. A sudden, fierce longing to go out and join the fun came over her. Instead, she gave a rueful glance at the cast on her foot. With her luck, she'd end up breaking another bone, more than likely in her neck this time.

The sledding halted when a snowball fight broke out. It quickly became father against daughters, and it was a pretty even fight as the snowballs flew fast and furious between them. Suddenly, a cry of pain brought the game to a halt. Sam quickly crossed to where one of the girls sat in the snow with her sister bending over her.

Sam pulled off his gloves and knelt in front of her. He pushed the brim of his hat back with one finger. "What's wrong, Lindy?"

"I hurt my eye," Lindy answered with a pout on her lips and one fist balled up against her face.

"Let me look." He tilted her face up and

carefully brushed the snow from her cheek. "I see it. There's an ouch-maker right here." He touched his lips in a gentle kiss to her eyelid. "Is that better?"

"No."

"It's not?" he asked in surprise. "I must be out of practice. My ouch-remover always works. Let me try again." He planted a second kiss on her cheek. "How's that?"

"That got it." She rubbed her eye and smiled at him.

"I think my eye hurts, too," Kayla said in a wistful voice.

"It does? Well, come here and let me see." Sam examined Kayla's eye critically and planted a kiss on her cheek, as well. "Better now?" he asked, and she nodded. "Good! Ready to fight some more?"

"No, we want to make snow angels."

"Grandma showed us how."

"Did she? You know what? She showed me how when I was about your age, too. Let me see if I remember." He flopped backward into the snow and began to swing his arms and legs and the twins quickly joined him.

Cheryl watched the scene from the balcony

door, and her heart warmed at the sight of Sam's tenderness. She remembered her own mother kissing her cheek to make the tears go away. It was a startling, clear and treasured memory of her mother, and Cheryl couldn't believe she'd forgotten it until now.

She stepped back and closed the door. Just for a moment, as she watched Sam and his children on the hillside, Cheryl wondered what her life would have been like if her father had been more like Sam. His children were very lucky, indeed.

Back in the bedroom, she sat down on the edge of the bed and picked up the phone. After dialing Damon's cell phone, she braced herself to give him the bad news.

He answered on the second ring. "Sands here."

"Damon, this is Cheryl."

"It's about time. Where are you?"

"Still stranded."

"What? Are you kidding?"

"No, and it only gets worse. I'm afraid my foot is broken. I'm not going to be able to rejoin you for a few weeks."

"Don't tell me that! Geoffrey is already

complaining because Miranda is taking your place in rehearsals. He says she outweighs you by ten pounds and his back is killing him from trying to lift her."

"He complains about my weight, too."

"I know, but you don't miss your jumps."

Cheryl cringed. "Did she?"

"The *jeté entrelacé,* twice! Fortunately, she recovered well. You understand I have to terminate your contract."

"Damon, please. I'll be back in a few weeks at most."

"Maybe! I can't hold your place. I'm sorry, Cheryl."

"But I need this job."

"It's too bad. You had potential."

It was the highest praise Damon had ever given her. She knew she wouldn't get anywhere by arguing with him. She was fired. The least she could do was take it with dignity. "I hope I have the honor of working with you again someday."

"We'll see. I've got to go. Give me your address so I can have your last check forwarded to you."

She gave him Sam's address then hung up

the phone and stared at it for a long time. The best role of her career had just gone down the drain. She knew there would be other roles, other chances to shine, but they seemed very far away at the moment. Now, what was she going to do in the meantime?

Several hours later, the tantalizing smell of roast beef drew her out of the book she'd been trying to read and out of the bedroom into the kitchen.

The twins were setting the table. One laid down the dishes, and the other followed arranging the flatware carefully beside each plate. Sam, wearing oversize orange oven mitts, removed a cookie sheet of golden-brown biscuits from the oven.

"Something smells wonderful," she said, maneuvering into the kitchen. The cast was heavy and her pain medicine left her feeling lightheaded and groggy. She joined Walter at the kitchen table, happy to have made it without falling.

Sam set the biscuits on a plate in the center of the table. "Are you feeling better? I could have brought you something to eat in bed. You didn't have to get up."

She smiled wanly. "I'm a little better, thank you. I wanted to get up. I'm not used to lying around."

"At least let me get that leg elevated. The doctor said you need to keep it up."

"Did he? I don't remember much after he set it."

Sam brought another chair and padded it with pillows, then gently lifted her foot onto it. The twins eyed them intently. He introduced them, and Cheryl had the feeling they hadn't told their father about meeting her earlier. She decided to keep mum as well and was rewarded with a grin from each of them. They came and sat on either side of her at the table.

Sam introduced the child on her left as Lindy, and the one on her right as Kayla. Cheryl tried to find some way to tell them apart, but she couldn't. They were dressed identically in blue jeans and green shirts.

The meal started out quietly, but the twins soon opened up and regaled her with stories of their stay at their grandmother's during the storm and of playing in the snow.

Eating at a tennis match would be easier,

Cheryl decided. They continued to start and finish each other's sentences on some hidden cue. She found she couldn't turn her head fast enough to keep up with them. Finally, she looked at Walter. "How do they do that?"

He shrugged. "Beats me."

"What do you do?" Lindy asked Cheryl.

"I'm a classical ballet dancer. A ballerina."

"Do you dance on your toes?" This time Kayla popped up with a question.

"Sometimes, but only when the steps of the dance call for it. Not all ballet is danced on your toes. There are lots of different steps."

"Do you wear a tutu?" Sam asked with a smirk.

Lifting her chin, she replied with a haughty air, "I wear many different costumes when I dance. Yes, I wear a tutu, but I have even worn a cowboy hat."

"Not in a ballet," Lindy jeered in disbelief.

Cheryl grew serious as she studied the girls' faces. "You've never been to a ballet, have you?"

Of course they hadn't. Neither had she at their age, and if it hadn't been for one special woman, Cheryl would have spent her whole life never knowing the beauty or her love of dancing. She glanced at Sam and Walter and wondered what they thought about her career. Did they consider it frivolous? And why should it matter what Sam or anyone else thought? It shouldn't, but for some reason, it did.

Focusing on the children, she began to explain her art. "Some ballets are written to express the joy of the dancing, and some tell a story, like *Cinderella* or *Peter and the Wolf.* In that ballet, I was the duck," she confided, and the girls giggled.

She stared at their father a long moment. "There is even a ballet about a lonely, clumsy cowgirl who wins the heart of the most handsome cowboy on the ranch. It's called *Rodeo.*"

She'd never had the role, but she knew exactly how the character would feel. Lonely and left out, sad and filled with a longing to be loved for who she was inside. Afraid no one could ever love her.

"Can you show us?" asked Kayla.

"What?" Momentarily lost in thought, Cheryl stared at the child.

"How to dance on our toes?" Lindy added.

Shaking her head, Cheryl said, "I'm afraid I can't. Not with my foot in a cast. Perhaps your father will take you to Kansas City someday and you can see a ballet there. There are several good companies there."

Kayla leaned forward. "Is that where you dance?"

"Cheryl is from New York, girls. That's much farther away than Kansas City. No, we can't go there and don't ask," Sam told them. "Enough questions. Eat!"

Cheryl, surprised to find her appetite returning, did justice to Sam's meal, including his light and fluffy biscuits. She sighed inwardly as she glanced across the table at him. He was a good cook and a devoted father. Neither of those were things she expected to find attractive in a man. Especially not a rancher. Somehow, she'd always thought that men who lived this life were hard and bitter. Like her father.

Instead, she was the one with bitterness in her heart. She didn't like deceiving Sam. He'd done so much for her already. Would he have been as helpful if he'd known who she really was? Maybe. Still, she should tell him. He deserved to know the truth. He looked up and their eyes met.

The air around her seemed to hum with a sudden intimacy.

Tell him who you are. Maybe he won't care.

As she stared at him, the friendliness of his gaze lightened her heart. Then she remembered the way other people had looked at her once they realized she was a Thatcher. The looks of condemnation—the looks of pity. Years of knowing people laughed at her behind her back, made fun of her, distrusted her, those feelings didn't go away simply because she wanted them to.

She looked away from Sam's gaze and struggled to quell the longings he kindled. She couldn't bear to see any of those emotions in his eyes.

She would be leaving soon. She would take her secrets with her and go back where no one knew anything about her past—a past she desperately wanted to forget.

To avoid Sam's scrutiny, she focused her attention on his children. As the meal progressed, she started to think she could detect a slight difference in mannerism between Lindy and Kayla. Lindy seemed more outgoing, a little brasher than her sister. Lindy's face was a little thinner, too. Cheryl directed several comments to the girls, and Lindy usually answered first.

Suddenly, Kayla dropped her spoon, and both girls piped up, "I'll get it!" They dived under the table together.

She heard giggling, but the children didn't reappear until Walter spoke. "Enough playing. Get up here and finish your meal."

They popped up and sat down in their chairs, but they continued to giggle. Sam tried to hide a grin, as well.

"What's going on here?" Cheryl asked with growing amusement. "If I had two shoes on, I would be looking to see if you'd tied my laces together."

"Oh, we wouldn't—" Kayla started.

"—do that," Lindy finished.

They ate the rest of their meal between giggles and grins, and as Cheryl studied their faces, she decided she had been mistaken. Kayla's face was slightly thinner.

When the meal was done, Sam stood and

consulted a list posted on the refrigerator door. "Lindy, it's your turn to load the dishwasher tonight."

With a small groan, the girl on Cheryl's right got up and began to clear the table. Bewildered, Cheryl said, "I thought you were Kayla?"

That brought a fresh outburst of laughter from the twins, and Cheryl looked at Sam. He couldn't keep a straight face.

"Oh, I get it, now," she said. "You two switched places under the table, didn't you?"

They nodded, and Cheryl shot Sam and Walter a stern look, but she couldn't maintain her stoic face, either. They all dissolved into laughter.

The rest of the evening she spent answering dozens of questions from the twins—about dancing, about her career and about New York City. Cheryl sat on the sofa with her foot propped up and answered their rapid-fire questions as best she could.

Walter had gone to his room, but Sam remained and looked on with an indulgent smile as they grilled her. He said, "Don't say I didn't warn you."

Cheryl didn't mind. She loved talking about the city and about her work. "These two should work for CNN. How many questions can they ask in an hour?"

"Enough to fill an encyclopedia. By the end of the night, I'll know everything there is to know about you."

Cheryl's grin faded. Not everything, she hoped.

"Do you have kids?" Lindy asked her.

"No, I don't."

The twins exchanged a knowing look, and Kayla said, "Are you married?"

"No."

Kayla glanced at her father and smiled in spite of the stern look he leveled at her. "Our dad's not married, either."

Cheryl sensed where they were going. She propped her elbow on the arm of the sofa and settled her chin on her hand. "I heard that."

Lindy grew serious. "Don't you think he's handsome?"

Cheryl tapped her fingers against her cheek and struggled not to laugh as Sam rolled his eyes. "He's sort of handsome."

"Would you like to have some kids?" They both looked at her with hopeful faces.

That threw her. The focus of her life had been dancing, to the exclusion of everything else. And yet, when she'd watched these two and Sam playing in the snow, she'd been filled with a longing to join in the fun, to become a part of something she didn't really understand—part of a family.

"I'm afraid I don't have time for a husband or for kids," she said at last. "I'm much too busy with my career."

The twins exchanged downcast looks.

Lindy recovered first from their setback. "Is it fun to be a dancer?"

Cheryl pondered the question. "It's very hard work. I have to practice for hours every day. Sometimes I even get hurt, and I still have to make myself go on. My boss—he's a choreographer, a person who designs a dance—he can be very tough. He's seldom happy with how our group performs, and he will make us do it over and over until he thinks it's right. But yes, it is fun."

She closed her eyes. "Sometimes when I'm dancing, the music catches me up and carries me along like a bit of thistledown on the wind. I can't describe it, really, but dancers call it *the float*. When I'm there, I forget how hard it is, and I only think about how much I love it."

Sam found his gaze riveted to Cheryl's face. She was an elegant, sophisticated woman. She glowed with excitement and happiness when she talked about her craft. "It's a great gift—to love the work you do."

She met his eyes. "A gift. I've never thought of it that way. Maybe that's true."

Sam cleared his throat. "Girls, it's bedtime."

"Not yet!" they pleaded.

"Yes, it is. You've had a long day."

"Can Cheryl read us a story?"

"Please, Daddy?" Lindy pleaded.

"I'd love to, if it's okay with you, Sam?"

"Please, Daddy?" Kayla added a soulful look.

"Okay." Sam watched as the twins gathered up the cat and headed for their room. "Can you make it down the stairs?" he asked Cheryl with a glance at her cast.

"Yes, cowboy. I can manage a few stairs."

"I was going to be gallant and offer to carry you."

"No. I think I'll be safer on my one good foot."

"Okay, but don't sue me if you fall."

The elegant, sophisticated woman stuck her tongue out, then followed the twins downstairs.

He would give anything to see her dance, Sam thought. The idea sobered him. She had devoted years of her life to the study and performance of an art he had barely acknowledged. He was attracted to her, yes, but it was useless to think it could lead to anything more. They didn't have anything in common.

He'd chosen the wrong kind of woman once. He wouldn't make that mistake again.

Cheryl managed the stairs without a mishap. The lower level of Sam's house was similar to the upper one, except the long room was a recreation room complete with a television, a billiard table and an assortment of games and toys for the children. Brown, overstuffed leather chairs sat grouped around a game table where a chess set waited for someone to finish a game.

The twins headed for one of the four doors along the back wall. "Here's our room," one of them announced.

It was Lindy who spoke, Cheryl decided, as she followed her into the room. Twin beds covered in spreads depicting rodeo scenes sat side by side. A pair of rocking horses stood stabled in one corner, decorated with carelessly thrown clothes, and an assortment of horse figurines lined up on the top of a bookshelf. Cheryl barely had time to glance around before the children urged her to see the next room.

"This is Gramps' room." Lindy held her fingers to her lips. "He says he goes to sleep early so he can get up with the chickens."

"That's funny 'cause we don't have any chickens," Kayla confessed.

Cheryl hid her grin with a hand to her mouth.

"This is the guest room," Kayla supplied, opening the next door. The room was decorated in the same Indian prints and bold patterns as the living room upstairs. The bed, neatly made, showed no sign that Sam had spent the night there.

The final door turned out to be Sam's office. Photographs of buildings both old and new as well as pictures of the twins decorated the walls. A large computer occupied a wide desk and rolled sheets of blueprints were neatly stored in deep bins. A drafting table held sketches of a beautiful stone-and-glass house. She had only a moment to admire the clean lines of the structure and to wonder what else he'd designed before the twins hurried her away.

They quickly got themselves ready for bed, dressing in matching pajamas.

Before her mother passed away Cheryl had believed in goodness. But when her mother died, what little goodness Cheryl knew died with her. Watching these two beautiful girls, she remembered.

Cheryl found it disturbing to think that the bad things in her life might have happened for a reason. Angie was happy now with a man who loved her. She said her tough childhood gave her a special insight into the children she wanted to help. Sam and his family were making Cheryl think about things she had ignored for years.

The girls presented Cheryl with a book. She read them their favorite story of Cinderella from the dog-eared copy. When she had finished, she tucked them in, wished them good-night and turned to leave.

"Wait." Lindy sat up in bed.

"Daddy always gives us a kiss," Kayla finished with a yawn.

"Like this?" Cheryl kissed the top of each head.

"Yup."

"Like that."

"I'm glad I got it right." Cheryl smiled softly as she turned off the light and left the room. Sam was waiting outside the door.

"I should be jealous." His voice, little more than a whisper, caused her pulse to take an erratic leap.

"Why?"

"They never go to bed that easily for me."

"I think you wore them out playing this afternoon."

"You might be right," he conceded with a grin.

"You have beautiful children, Sam. You're a lucky man."

"I think so, too," he answered quietly.

Suddenly, she realized how close he stood. His eyes roved over her face as though he were trying to memorize each feature. She stared for a long moment into his dark eyes. If only things were different. Why wish for such a foolish thing?

"We think she's beautiful, Daddy," a little voice said.

"Don't you think she is?"

Cheryl felt the heat of a blush steal up her cheeks.

Sam looked down at the big eyes of his daughters as they peeked out the crack of their bedroom door. He tried for a stern, fatherly tone but didn't quite make it.

"I think she's very pretty." His mouth twitched as he tried not to smile. "What are you doing out of bed?"

"You didn't kiss us good-night," Lindy reminded him.

"Back to bed, both of you. I'll be in soon."

"After you kiss Cheryl good-night?"

"Close the door, now!"

It snapped shut. He stepped back a pace and shoved his hands in his pockets. "I'm sorry about that."

"It's okay. They mean well. Good night, Sam."

Sam pushed a hand through his hair as he watched her climb the stairs. He'd always considered himself a smart man, but he sure wasn't acting like it where she was concerned. He knew better than to get involved with her. By her own admission, her career was more important than a husband or a family.

He glanced toward the closed bedroom door. Silently, he vowed to remember that his children were the most important people in his life. They needed good examples, good role models to follow. As much as he felt drawn to Cheryl, she wasn't what he or his girls needed.

Chapter Seven

Cheryl tried to concentrate on the book she was reading, but it was useless. She prided herself on being levelheaded, on her ability to stay focused on her career. She had never let a man interfere with her desire to be a successful dancer. Yet, her career was something that seemed to slip to the back of her mind when Sam Hardin was around. He scrambled her common sense without even trying. One glimpse of his endearing, lopsided grin, and her insides turned to jelly.

Glancing out the window, she watched low gray clouds scuttle across the prairie sky. The wind that drove them today was a warm south wind and the snow was melting rapidly. Soon, she'd be able to disappear as fast. The thought brought an ache to her heart as real as the ache in her broken foot.

Sam had pleaded work as his excuse and vanished downstairs after breakfast. He'd been down there most of the afternoon. Supposedly, he was working on finding a nanny to take care of the children while his mother was gone.

The twins were playing downstairs, and occasionally the sound of their voices floated up the stairwell. Their happy chatter filled the house with a pleasant hubbub.

Cheryl picked up her book and tried to concentrate again, but when she found herself reading the same page over for the third time, she put it down with disgust. From the corner of her eye, she spied Bonkers walking around the end of the sofa, and she did a double take.

The cat strolled through the living room dressed in a pink, ruffled, baby dress with little puffy sleeves. His outfit was complete with ruffled underpants that had a hole cut out for his tail. A pink bonnet tied in a lopsided bow beneath his chin was the crowning touch. Cheryl couldn't help herself—she burst out laughing.

Bonkers paused in his trek across the room, gave her a malevolent stare, then slipped beneath the sofa. A moment later, the twins came pounding up the stairs and piled to a stop in front of Cheryl. She still wasn't sure which one was which.

"Our baby is missing."

"Have you seen him?"

Cheryl pointed downward. "I believe he's under the sofa, girls."

They dropped to the floor and peered beneath it.

"Yup, he's under there."

"I think he's mad at us."

"I told you he didn't want baby lotion on his tail, Lindy." Kayla's scolding clued Cheryl into which one was speaking.

"You did not."

"Did, too!"

"Did not!"

"All right, now," Cheryl intervened. "Bonkers will come out when he's ready."

The twins climbed on the sofa beside her.

"I was only trying to be a good mommy. I didn't know it would make him mad," Lindy confessed with a long face.

"I'm sure he won't stay mad, sweetheart. And I think you will be a great mommy," Cheryl tried to console her.

"Our mommy was a bad mommy," Lindy said.

Dumbfounded, Cheryl stared at her. "What do you mean?"

"Our mommy didn't want us," Kayla answered sadly.

"She gave us away," Lindy added with a dramatic sigh.

"Just like kittens stuffed in a sack."

"Who said that?" Cheryl demanded.

Kayla exchanged a glance with her sister. "Jimmy Slader's mom."

"She didn't think we were listening," Lindy added.

"Merci Slader?" Cheryl asked in disbelief.

Both girls nodded.

Cheryl hesitated, uncertain of how to proceed. Having a serious conversation with two five-year-olds was a little out of her league. More than that, she felt she shouldn't be prying into Sam's private life.

"What has your father told you about why your mother doesn't live with you?" she asked gently.

"He said they both loved us," Kayla volunteered.

"But they didn't want to be married anymore," Lindy added.

"Mommy wanted to marry someone else and live far away."

"And Daddy wanted to live on the ranch."

"So they chose the bestest place for us to live."

"Here with Daddy," Lindy concluded.

A simplified answer for a marital breakup, but Cheryl wasn't about to delve into anything more complicated. "I think your dad would tell you the truth."

"I think so, too," Lindy declared.

"Besides, I don't remember being in a sack," Kayla added.

Lindy crossed her arms. "Me, neither!"

Cheryl fought back a smile. "I think Jimmy Slader's mom may be full of hot air."

The twins giggled, but Kayla grew somber

again. "Is it okay if I still love Mommy, even if she didn't want us?"

"No, you can't!" Lindy shouted. "I told you that!"

Cheryl gathered them close in a quick, impulsive hug. "Yes, you can, darling. It's okay to love her."

She struggled to find the right words. "When someone you love does something bad, you don't have to like what they've done, but you can still love that person." Her father's and her brother's faces came to mind, and she realized the truth of what she was saying. She knew her dad hadn't been much of a father, but she'd never stopped loving him, never stopped trying to earn his love in return, even though she knew the things he did were wrong. And she'd never stopped loving Jake even after all this time.

She gazed down at the children. "Do you understand what I'm trying to say?"

"I think so," Kayla said.

"Maybe." Lindy sounded reluctant to agree.

Cheryl smiled softly. "I'll bet Jimmy Slader loves his mother, even though she's full of hot air."

They both grinned, then Lindy said, "Daddy says she wants to take care of us when he can't be here."

Kayla crossed her arms and looked sullen. "Until Grandma comes back."

"'Cause he has to go to Kansas City, and we can't go with him."

"But we don't want her. So he's gonna find—"

"—a ninny to take care of us."

Cheryl struggled to keep a straight face with difficulty. "I think you mean a nanny."

Kayla gave a sharp nod. "Yup, that's what we said."

Cheryl caught a quick look that flashed between the two of them. Suddenly, she had the feeling she was being set up.

Lindy looked at her with beseeching brown eyes. "Why don't you stay and take care of us until Grandma comes back?"

"We like you," Kayla added sincerely.

Cheryl discovered something new about children then. Even when you knew you were being wheedled, it didn't keep you from wanting to give in. It tugged at her heart that they would ask her to stay, and she felt like a heel for rejecting their offer.

"I can't. The only reason I haven't left already is because I haven't been able to find my wallet. I lost it out in the snow after my accident, but the snow is almost gone now, and your father will be able to find it soon, and then I have to leave."

"But you can't dance with your foot broken. You said so," Lindy argued.

"I know, but if I'm lucky, I can get a job helping take care of costumes or the sets. Ballet is what I do." She stroked a hand through each set of downy curls. "Like your dad takes care of the ranch and builds houses. It's my job."

"But why?" they pleaded.

Cheryl didn't quite know how to convey the meaning of the word *career* to them. "When you dress Bonkers up in baby clothes, that doesn't make him a real baby, does it? He's still a cat."

She paused to see if they understood what she was saying. "Right now I may not seem like a ballerina, but inside I am. It's all I've ever wanted to be."

The two faces watching her grew sadder

with each word she spoke. Their solemn eyes filled with tears.

"You just don't like us," Kayla said mournfully.

"That's not true," Cheryl insisted.

Bonkers sprang up beside them on the sofa. His bonnet hung from his neck by a shredded ribbon. Lindy gathered up her make-believe baby, and the girls climbed down. Cheryl reached out to stop them, but Bonkers flattened his ears and hissed at her, and she snatched her hand back.

Sam stood at the top of the stairs as the somber-faced pair marched around him without a word. Cheryl cast him a pleading glance, but he shook his head. "You have only known them for two days. I've had to cope with them for five years, and they still do it to me. Welcome to the Giant Rat Fink Club."

"If those two don't end up on the stage, the world will be denied the presence of great actresses," Cheryl said in awe.

"I hate to tell you this, New York, but they're just getting started."

He walked over and sat beside her on the sofa. "I have to admit, it's a good idea. I'm sure I can't pay you what a ballerina earns. In spite of appearances, ranching isn't always a prosperous business, but I think I can pay you what a ninny would make."

They exchanged amused glances. "I think you have an exaggerated idea of what a ballerina pulls down," she said. "It's a tempting offer, Sam, but no."

"You said yourself that you can't dance. This way you have a place to stay and a little money coming in until your foot is healed."

"Sam, I can't. I adore your kids, but I have to rejoin my company."

He grew serious as he studied her face. He reached out and brushed a wisp of hair back from the edge of her jaw, then dropped his hand. He stood and smiled at her. "I hate to think you're leaving us for a bunch of guys in pink tights."

A grin struggled through her sadness. Trust Sam to find a way to make her smile.

He gave a nod in the direction of the stairs. "I've got to get back to work now. Is there anything I can do for you?"

"No, I'm fine."

"Do you think you could stay until Friday

at least? I really do need to go to Kansas City on Thursday. If I can convince these clients to go with my design, it'll mean a lot. It seems the girls aren't crazy about Merci's offer to let them stay with her. Walter thinks he can handle them, but the truth is, I'd feel better if I had someone to look after all of them."

"I'll stay until then," she conceded. "It's the least I can do after all you've done for me. Besides, I can't go anywhere until I have my wallet back, or until I know for sure I need to report everything as lost."

"Thanks. Most of the snow is gone. I'll go look for it again this afternoon," he offered, turning to leave.

"Thanks, Sam." Cheryl watched him walk back to the staircase. His broad shoulders slumped as he thrust his hands deep in his pockets. Watching him walk away, she had the strangest feeling that she'd just lost something very valuable, and it wasn't her wallet.

Sam checked on the twins, but they weren't in their room. It wasn't unusual for them to retreat to the barn or the garden when they were unhappy. He'd talk to them about Cheryl's leaving later.

Back in his office, he sat down at his desk, dropped his head onto both hands and raked his fingers through his hair. All he had to do was find a way to tell the twins they couldn't have what he wanted, too. For Cheryl to stay.

He reminded himself once again that this attraction couldn't go anywhere. She was the exact opposite of what he needed. He needed a woman who wanted to be a mother to his children. Cheryl was beautiful, funny and intelligent, but she wasn't interested in being a mother, or in living on a ranch. She had a life planned that was far different. A life he and his children could have no part in.

An hour later, he heard the twins return. He opened their bedroom door to find two muddy and tired girls. They nodded quietly when he told them Cheryl wouldn't be staying. The arguments he expected didn't materialize. He left their room feeling a little worried and more than a bit suspicious of such cooperative behavior.

The weather warmed up to its normal springtime high the next day. By afternoon, the snow was gone except for a few drifts that lingered in the shade of the buildings and trees.

By mutual and unspoken consent, Sam and Cheryl avoided any talk of her leaving. Cheryl expected the time to pass awkwardly but was surprised to find that she enjoyed a growing friendship with Sam. If her smiles were too bright, or her humor a little forced, no one seemed to notice. When she found herself longing for something more, she ruthlessly pushed those feelings aside. And if she wasn't sleeping well, she put it down to her aching foot.

The twins were treating her like royalty, she noted, as they carefully carried her lunch tray out onto the balcony for an impromptu picnic on the second day of beautiful weather. The snow was gone from the hillside where she had watched them sledding. Here and there, hardy spring flowers that had been hidden by the snow were putting in an appearance.

Cheryl was enjoying her time with the girls when the sound of footsteps caused her heart to flutter and skip a beat. Sam came up the stairs that led to the balcony from a walk at the side of the house.

"Am I too late for lunch?" he asked.

"Nope, you're just in time." Lindy presented him with a messy version of a peanut butter and jelly sandwich. "I made it myself," she announced proudly.

Cheryl had already sampled hers. She watched Sam take a seat and tip his hat back.

"This is what I like," he stated cheerfully.

"Peanut butter and jelly?" Cheryl inquired with a raised eyebrow.

"Nope. Having lunch with three pretty ladies." He drew smiles from all the ladies with his blatant flattery and took a hearty bite of his sandwich. He had a little jelly left on the side of his mouth when he finished, and Cheryl found herself holding his chin steady to wipe it off with her napkin. His teasing grin faded, and his eyes darkened. She let her hand fall back to the table and looked away.

Across from them the twins glanced at each other and smiled slyly. "Can we go play?"

"Sure," Sam answered absently, and they took off.

Easy, Sam, he cautioned himself. *You can be friends, but nothing more.* He tried to concentrate on something besides the way she made him wish she wasn't the wrong woman for him.

"The girls really like you," he said. "Not many people can learn to tell them apart as quickly as you have."

"I adore them. They're as bright as new pennies. You've done a fine job with them, Sam."

"Thanks. You should have kids of your own. You're great with them." He dropped his gaze to his plate. That was a stupid thing to say. He must be as transparent as glass, but what would it hurt to put the idea out and see how she reacted? He held his breath as he waited for her reply.

"Maybe I will. Someday. Who knows?"

Sam's hope rose. It wasn't a flat no. If only they had more time.

She smiled at him brightly. "I'd just have to meet the right man first."

"And what would the right man be like?"

"Oh, someone who loves ballet and hot pretzels with mustard and New York City even in the summer when it's muggy and clogged with smog."

"I thought maybe it would be a guy who brought you chocolate and roses?"

She looked away and didn't answer. Sam rose to his feet. He had to stop kidding himself, she'd never be happy here.

"I've got a council member meeting tonight and Walter has his weekly checkers game with one of our neighbors. Do you think you can handle the terrible twosome by yourself for an evening?"

She smiled and nodded. "No problem, cowboy. Just leave me the phone number where you'll be, the hospital's number—" she began to count off on her fingers "—the sheriff's number, poison control, the fire department, ah, your insurance agent's number, the number for your next of kin, the vet's number…"

"The vet?"

"In case anything happens to Bonkers."

"Aren't we being a little paranoid?"

"Good idea. Leave me your therapist's number."

"I don't have a therapist. But I'm beginning to think I may need one. Oh, I almost forgot.

This letter came for you today." He pulled a folded white envelope from his shirt pocket and handed it to her.

"That must be my last paycheck." Cheryl took it and tucked it in her shirt pocket. She would look at it later. That way if she burst into tears at the tiny amount no one would see her.

Later that day, as she watched Sam let his daughters help with the housework, she realized that he loved being a father. He was endlessly patient with the girls' less-than-perfect efforts, and Cheryl found herself admiring his kindness and the gentle way he helped tiny hands perform eager tasks.

For ten years Cheryl had been consumed by her work. Now, everything she'd denied she needed was suddenly spread out before her, and she was disturbed to feel she'd been missing out on something equally as important as her dancing.

Her evening alone with the twins went smoothly. Later that night, she remembered her paycheck and pulled it out of her pocket. When she opened the envelope there wasn't a check. There was only a single sheet of paper without a signature. On it in bold block print was written,

Go away. You aren't wanted here. Go away.

The terse missive made Cheryl's skin crawl. Who had sent it? Who wanted her gone? She picked up the envelope, but there was no return address. It seemed that she had made someone angry. Merci perhaps? Who else could it be?

The troubling letter kept her awake long after she lay in bed. Sleep eluded her as she listened for the sound of Sam coming home and wondered what she should do about the note. There really was nothing to do, she realized. She would be leaving soon. Only, she didn't like the idea that someone would think she had turned tail and run away after a sick prank like this.

It was after midnight when she finally heard Sam's truck in the driveway, followed by his quiet footsteps across the hardwood floor in the living room. She turned over and settled his pillow under her face, but sleep was a long time in coming.

The following day, between the insistent twins and the lure of the warm sunshine, Cheryl decided to venture out and explore some of the ranch. Once outside, the twins headed for the large red barn and white painted corrals across the gravel yard. A windmill twirled gaily beside the barn. The breeze that spun it brought the loamy scent of spring to her, and Cheryl was surprised to discover how much she'd missed the enticing freshness and smells of a Kansas spring.

Sam stood saddling a tall, roan horse beside the barn. He wore a light blue denim shirt, jeans and leather chaps. His high-heeled boots sported blunt silver spurs. The fringe of his chaps fluttered softly as he moved. The man was a cowgirl's dream come to life, she thought, as she watched him lift the heavy saddle with ease. He spoke softly to the big roan as he bent to reach under the horse's belly for the girth. Too bad she wasn't a cowgirl.

Sam lowered the stirrup after he'd finished

tightening the cinch and patted the roan's shoulder. The horse, meanwhile, had his head down allowing the twins to scratch enthusiastically behind his ears.

"Come on, Cheryl, come see our new baby calf," Kayla insisted. The girls took off toward a second, smaller corral.

Cheryl smiled at Sam and willed her heart to stop its wild fluttering as she followed the pair to where a little Charolais was busy suckling lunch from his patient mother. His stubby tail was twirling nearly as fast as the windmill. Every now and then, he gave his mother's udder an impatient butt with his snowy head.

"Wait a minute," Sam called. He mounted and rode up beside them. "Grandpa Walter has gone into town for feed, so you girls will be on your own while I'm gone. It's okay if you want to pet Henrietta's new calf, she won't mind, but don't go into the other corral. I opened the barn door so Harvey can come out now that the weather's getting warmer. You stay out of his corral. Is that understood?" His tone was stern.

"Yes, sir!" rang out from all three of them.

"Good." He grinned at Cheryl's mock salute.

"Who's Harvey?" she asked.

"Possibly the salvation of this ranch."

"I don't understand."

"He's one of those pedigreed cattle I was talking about. Harvey is our three-time-grand-champion Charolais show bull and the backbone of our advanced breeding program. There are cows lined up as far away as Canada who are just waiting to have one of his calves."

Cheryl wrinkled her nose. "He's going to be busy, isn't he?"

"Very busy, I hope." Sam grinned at her, touched the brim of his hat, then whirled his horse and rode away.

She watched him ride out of the yard. It wasn't fair. The man looked even better on horseback.

The twins leaned through the fence and began petting the calf's wooly head when he paused in his eating to investigate these potential new playmates. He frisked away from the twins, and the girls slipped through the fence to follow him in an impromptu game of tag.

Cheryl glanced toward the barn. A small white cat, followed by a trio of black-and-white kittens intent on catching their mother's twitching tail, emerged to sit in a patch of sunshine. Cheryl looked for a bull but didn't see him.

It was foolish to worry about a cat that obviously lived in the barn, but she didn't want the kittens playing in harm's way.

"Here kitty, kitty," she called, extending her hand. The next instant, the bull's massive head appeared in the doorway. He dwarfed the kittens clustered beneath him. Cheryl held her breath, certain she was about to see them trampled.

She checked quickly for the twins. They were still in the adjacent pen. They stood looking into a large round stock tank. It extended under both sides of the corral fence so animals in both enclosures could drink from it. Cheryl didn't think they could see the kittens.

She looked back at the gigantic white bull. He snorted once over the kittens, but the silly things didn't have the sense to run. Then, he put his muzzle down and snorted again. One kitten merely arched its back and rubbed against the giant's nose. With a gentle push Cheryl wouldn't have believed if she hadn't seen it, the bull moved the kittens out of his way, stepped out into the sunshine and lumbered across the corral.

He was a magnificent animal. Dense white ringlets covered his head and thick neck, and his snowy coat gleamed in the sunlight. Powerful muscles moved smoothly as he trotted around the perimeter of the corral.

"Cheryl, look what we can do," Lindy called.

The twins had climbed to the top of the fence and begun to walk along it with their arms outstretched like tightrope walkers. It was a game Cheryl and her sister had played often as children. The object was to see who could walk the thick wooden rail the farthest without falling.

The bull took an interest in their activity and moved to stand beside the tank as the girls walked over the top of it. With the huge animal standing so close, suddenly, the children's game didn't look so safe. Cheryl moved down the fence toward them. She wanted to call out, but she was afraid to startle the girls.

Lindy reached the far side of the tank and jumped down with a laugh. Cheryl let out a sigh of relief, then everything happened at once.

Lindy's jump startled the bull. He swung his head against the boards with a blow that shook the entire fence. Kayla lost her balance, uttering a short, bitten-off scream as she fell. Her head struck the steel rim of the tank as her body disappeared with a splash.

Cheryl screamed Kayla's name and lunged to grip the fence in front of her. Lindy's scream echoed her own.

Sam was headed down the lane when he heard the screams. He turned in the saddle in time to see Cheryl throw her crutch over the corral fence and vault over after it.

He couldn't believe his eyes. She fell once, came up with her crutch and continued to charge across the muddy pen sending the cow and calf bolting out of her way. Sam searched for the twins, but he saw only one child standing beside the stock tank screaming.

He ruthlessly hauled his horse's head around and spurred for the corrals.

Chapter Eight

Cheryl reached the stock tank and gripped the cold metal rim. There was no sign of Kayla. Quickly, she stepped into the icy, hip-deep water and began searching by feel under the murky surface.

"Kayla, where are you, baby?" Cheryl heard the panic in her own voice.

Unable to locate Kayla on the side where she had fallen, Cheryl took a deep breath and ducked under the fence that divided the tank. Her fingers touched a small hand. Quickly, she pulled the child to her and stood. Water streamed down her face as she gasped for air, but she cradled Kayla's limp body against her chest.

Sam galloped into the yard and reined his horse to a sliding stop beside the corral. He kicked free of the stirrups, vaulted out of the saddle and over the fence in a single movement and hit the ground running.

Cheryl slogged through the water and handed Kayla into his reaching arms. He took the child and gently laid her on the ground.

"She was on the fence," Cheryl panted. "She fell and hit her head."

Stepping out of the water, she knelt beside him. "I couldn't find her, Sam. It took so long."

Kayla's lips were blue, her skin translucent and pale as marble.

Cheryl felt for a pulse in the child's neck. *Please, let her be okay.* To her relief, she found one, strong and steady beneath her fingers. The faint rise and fall of her little chest confirmed she was breathing. "She has a good pulse."

Sam's own heart began to beat again. "Kayla, wake up, kitten. Can you hear me?"

Kayla's eyelids fluttered open, and she

slowly focused on his face. "Daddy?" she whispered.

It was the sweetest sound he'd ever heard. He lifted her small body and cradled her close. "Yes, baby, Daddy's here." His voice broke, and he rocked her gently.

Wiping the tears from his face, he looked at Cheryl. "Thank you." He stretched out his hand. She grasped it firmly.

"Daddy, is Kayla okay?"

Sam took one look at Lindy's frightened face and pulled her close to her sister in his arms.

Cheryl said, "She hit her head pretty hard when she fell, Sam. I think we should get her to the hospital."

She was right. Reluctantly, he handed his daughter to her and stood. He was surprised to find his knees wouldn't hold him, and he staggered slightly as his head spun. Bending over, he braced his hands on his thighs and took several deep breaths. When his head stopped spinning, he tried to marshal his thoughts. "I'll go get the truck."

"Get a blanket first. She's freezing."

"So are you." He turned and hurried toward

the house. As he set one boot on the fence, he paused and looked back. Cheryl knelt on the muddy ground with Kayla cradled across her lap, her soft voice reassuring both girls.

The cow and its calf had come up behind her and watched the proceedings with bovine inquisitiveness. Lowering her head, the cow sniffed at Kayla's face. Cheryl pushed the animal aside with an indifferent shove, as if she'd handled cattle all her life. Sam wasn't sure why, but the sight triggered a touch of unease in his mind. There was more to Cheryl Steele than she let on.

Sitting wrapped in a blanket in Sam's pickup, Cheryl held Kayla on her lap as they sped toward the hospital. Kayla lay pale and quiet, but her breathing was regular. Cheryl kept one hand inside the blanket just to make sure. She'd known these children only a few days, but already they'd wormed their way firmly into her heart.

Lindy sat between the adults on the seat. "I think me and Kayla got mixed up," she said in a faltering voice.

Puzzled, Cheryl glanced at Sam, but he

seemed bewildered, as well. Cheryl slipped an arm around Lindy's shoulders and drew her close. "What do you mean, honey?"

"When you do something bad, you get punished. But me and Kayla mixed up."

"Sweetheart," Sam said. "It was an accident."

"Even if we did something bad?"

"Your daddy is right, Lindy. It was a scary accident, that's all. Will it make you feel better to tell us what you think you did?"

Lindy nodded. "We found your wallet, and we hid it so you couldn't go away," her voice tapered off into a little whisper.

Cheryl was speechless.

Sam shook his head. "I should have known you two were up to something.

Wiggling free of Cheryl's hold, Lindy snuggled up against him. "Are you mad? It was my idea," she confessed with more resolve.

Draping an arm over her shoulder, he pulled her against him. "I'm disappointed that you thought you could make Cheryl stay by keeping something that belonged to her, but

I'm not angry with you. I love you. Do you understand?"

Lindy nodded. "Cheryl told us you can love somebody even if they do bad things."

Sam met Cheryl's gaze over his daughter's head. "Did she?"

"Yup," Lindy answered.

"She's a smart lady."

Cheryl basked in the glow of his praise for only a moment. Then the reality of what had happened sank in. She should have been watching the girls more closely. She should have made them get down the second she saw what they were doing. This was her fault.

Why hadn't her mother been saved the way Kayla just was? Was one life less valuable than the other? She had no answers for the questions that spun through her mind. She rode the rest of the way in silence.

In the E.R., Sam stayed with Kayla while Cheryl was taken to have her foot looked at. Her cast was a water-logged mass of plaster. Dr. Carlton proceeded to scold her for using her foot, X-rayed it and applied a new cast. When he was finished, he held open the door of the exam room, and Cheryl maneuvered herself out on her crutches.

"There doesn't seem to be any damage to the healing bones," he informed her. "This is a walking cast I've put on. It is not a running, jumping or dancing cast, understood? I don't want you putting your full weight on that foot yet. Use the crutches for another two weeks, then a cane if it's comfortable."

She listened with only half an ear as he gave instructions to a petite, dark-haired nurse. When he turned back, he said, "I wish I could place where I know you from, young lady."

"Maybe she just looks like someone you know," his nurse suggested.

Cheryl tensed. She'd been told she looked like her mother. Could he have known Mira?

"Maybe. It'll come to me," he said.

"Where's Kayla now?" Cheryl asked, eager to see her.

"I'll find out for you," the nurse answered.

Cheryl was given the room number, then made her way down the hospital corridor. At Kayla's door, she paused. A sign said visitors were limited to family only. Should she go in?

Family or not, she needed to know for herself that Kayla was okay. She put her hand on the door.

"You can't go in there."

Cheryl turned to see Merci Slader coming down the hall.

"Hospital policy—family only," Merci said, stopping beside Cheryl. "Kayla is fine. I just checked with her nurse. Actually, I'm a bit surprised that you're still here. I thought you'd be on your way by now."

"I'll leave when I'm ready, Merci." She considered confronting the woman about the letter, but decided against it. There were more important things to think about. Like Kayla.

"I think the sooner you move on the better it will be for everyone. I know Sam thought you could help watch the girls, but obviously you can't do that in your condition. Isn't this terrible accident proof of that?" With a smug parting smile, she left.

Cheryl watched Merci go, then squared her shoulders. She needed to see Kayla, and she wasn't about to let Merci Slader or a few puny hospital rules stop her. She pushed open the door.

Inside, she found Sam seated beside Kayla's bed with Lindy curled up in his lap. He had one arm stretched over the metal rail, and he stroked Kayla's dark curls as she lay on the pristine sheets. She looked terribly small and helpless.

Sam spoke as Cheryl came and stood beside him. "Kayla, baby. Cheryl's here."

Kayla opened sleepy eyes and smiled up at Cheryl. "Hi."

"Hi yourself, Tweedledee. How are you feeling?"

"Okay."

Lindy leaned toward the bed and touched her sister's face. "I told them," she whispered.

Kayla's lip quivered and tears filled her eyes as she focused on Cheryl. "Are you gonna leave now? Please, don't go. We want you to take care of us!"

Sam tried to comfort her, but she continued to cry and plead. He sent Cheryl an imploring look and she understood. Kayla needed to stay calm and to rest.

"I'll stay as long as you need me." Planting a kiss on Kayla's brow, she added, "Why don't you try and sleep now?"

Kayla sniffled. "You won't leave until I'm asleep, will you?"

"No. I promise."

"Okay. Daddy, can Lindy sleep with me?"

"Sure." Sam settled Lindy in the bed with her sister. They snuggled together and Kayla slept at last.

Cheryl moved away from the bed and spoke in a low voice. "I'm so sorry, Sam. I should have been keeping a better eye on them."

"Hush. It wasn't your fault. I've told them a dozen times not to walk on the top of the fences. Besides, you saved her life." Sam drew her into his arms and settled his chin on top of her head as he held her close.

She relished the strength and the feeling of safety his embrace gave her. She rested against his tall, strong body, gathering comfort from his arms around her. It felt so right. She had promised to stay as long as Kayla needed her, but what on earth was she getting herself into?

Sam held her away and looked into her eyes. "Have I said thank-you?"

"You're welcome," she whispered, gazing at him. He was everything her heart needed. His touch sent her senses singing with happiness. Before she knew what to expect, he bent his head and kissed her. The warmth of his lips spread to the center of her chest and sent her heart racing with delight.

A knock on the door brought her back to earth, and she quickly stepped away as Walter poked his head in.

Sam let Cheryl go reluctantly. He wanted her back in his arms, but instead, he spoke to his obviously worried grandfather. "Come in, Gramps."

"I got your message and came as quick as I could. How is she?" He moved to the bedside and reached a trembling hand down to caress Kayla's hair.

"The doctor wants to keep her overnight for observation. Her lungs are clear. She's got a goose-egg-size lump on the back of her head, but nothing's broken."

"Good."

"It could have been so much worse."

"I've outlived my wife and my son. I sure don't want to outlive my great-granddaughter."

Cheryl laid a comforting hand on the old man's arm. He squeezed it in return, then wiped at his eyes. "What do you need me to do, Sammy?"

Sam rubbed a weary hand over his face. "I'll spend the night here. Could you drive Cheryl back to the ranch?"

"No. Let me stay," Cheryl pleaded.

"Look, why don't we do this," Walter suggested. "I'll stay with the girls while you take Cheryl home, and you can change." He gave Sam a wry smile as he looked him up and down. "I hate to bring it up, but you smell a bit ripe."

Sam looked down at his boots and jeans. Gramps was right. He hadn't paid the least bit of attention to what he knelt in when he'd laid Kayla down in the corral. He grimaced and said, "You always said it's the smell of money."

Walter gave him a little push to get him started toward the door. "Every rancher says that. Go home and come back when you smell broke. I'll be here if the girls need anything."

"Okay, you win. Thanks." With a glance at the sleeping twins, he allowed Cheryl and himself to be herded out the door.

* * *

Cheryl paused as she entered the quiet house. It echoed with emptiness. The children added the life that made it home. The thought brought her up short. When had she started thinking of this place as home? It wasn't. It could never be. Not for her.

She changed while Sam went to shower, then she retrieved her wallet from under Lindy's pillow. Slowly, she made her way upstairs, sat on the sofa and laid her head back with a weary sigh. She had been a fool to promise Kayla she would stay longer. Every day she remained here she risked being exposed. She didn't want her past laid bare before Sam and his family. She cared about them. She wasn't the same angry, foolhardy girl who had caused so much harm all those years ago.

Raising her fingertips to her temples, she tried to massage away her dull headache. What was she doing getting more involved with this family? It didn't take a genius to see that Sam and the children were growing fond of her. That she returned their regard didn't change things. She wasn't being fair to them by building up their hopes that she would stay.

Feeling tired but restless, she rose and opened the sliding glass door to the balcony and took a deep breath of fresh air. The soft evening breeze toyed with her hair as she stepped out and sat on the glider. Quietly, she rocked and watched as the sunset colored the timeless hills in shades of rose, lavender and gold.

She wasn't given much to introspection, Cheryl realized. She looked forward—never back. The past was too painful. She'd spent her whole life being ashamed of what her father and her half brother had done, what they'd made her a part of. She came to hate this land—the treeless, windswept hills where her mother and her childhood had both died painful deaths.

Gazing out at hills rolling away to the horizon, Cheryl slowly understood it had been the events that she hated, not this place.

These hills were a part of her. She knew the call of the meadowlark and the cry of the hawk that rode the wind in lazy circles across a flawless blue sky. She knew the ceaseless wind that sent the long grasses bowing before it in undulating waves. Her soul heard the music the wind played in the grass just as surely as she heard it when she danced.

The balcony door opened, but she didn't turn around. Dusk was fading and the evening stars began to shine in the darkening heavens. These hills may have been her home once, but not anymore. She wasn't strong enough to face the prejudice and shame all over again. The thought of Sam finding out what she had done sent a chill racing down her spine.

He sat beside her and slipped an arm around her shoulder. She wanted to lean against him, to draw comfort from his strength and warmth, but she didn't. Silently, she watched the stars come out, one by one.

She was so close to falling in love with this man. The earthy, masculine scent of him filled her with hopes and dreams she didn't fully understand. The tender way he stroked her hair left her feeling strangely content. It would be so easy to let herself love him.

She was already half in love with his daughters. Lindy and Kayla had crept into her heart when she wasn't looking. Somewhere between trading places under the table and the near tragedy today, they had opened her eyes to the joys of having children be a part of her life.

Until today, she had believed that to dance was all she needed. The grueling work, the pain and the joy of the dance was what she lived for. It was an all-consuming life because she wanted it that way. On the stage, people admired her for what she could do, for her talent, not for who she was inside. She didn't believe that she deserved someone to love and to be loved by in return.

Now, Sam and the children were showing her a different kind of life. A life where family came first. Where people worked together because they loved each other, not because they had to. But that life shimmered just beyond her reach—because she couldn't stay.

She was risking discovery, but more than that, she was risking a terrible heartache. Staying was out of the question. She would remain until she was certain Kayla was all right, then she'd leave. Sam's arm tightened around her shoulders.

"Are you okay?" he asked.

"Just tired," she said quickly. Somehow, she had to find the strength to harden her heart against this longing to stay in his arms.

She moved out of his embrace, stood and pushed her hair back as she tried for a nonchalant tone. "I must say, cowboy, this place has supplied me with more excitement in one week than I've had in the last ten years. I don't know how you stand it."

He cleared his throat. "Yeah. It's been one tough day. Are you sure you're okay?"

She nodded as she moved away from him to stand at the balcony rail.

Sam felt empty and cold without her warmth against his side. He wanted her back in his arms. She had saved his child's life, and he was indebted to her, but it wasn't gratitude he felt when he held her. It was much more, yet he found it hard to trust his feelings. It was harder still to put them into words. He'd been wrong about a woman once before. What if he was wrong again?

How did Cheryl feel about what was happening between them? He wanted to ask, but maybe this wasn't the right time. "I guess we've both had a little too much excitement," he said.

She gave him a weak smile before she turned back to stare out into the night. "That's for sure. I'll be glad to get back to New York where life is safe and calm. It's been fun, cowboy, but I can't take much more of this."

There was his answer—she couldn't wait to leave. "I'm sorry you had to lie."

She spun toward him, her face pale in the starlight. "What do you mean?"

"When you told Kayla you would stay."

"Oh, that."

"What did you think I meant?"

"Nothing. It wasn't a lie. I will stay until she's better."

"What if someone else asks you to stay? Would you consider it?" His slender stalk of hope wouldn't die. He waited, afraid to breathe. He almost missed her soft whisper.

"I would have to say—no."

Disappointment burned itself deep in his heart. Turning away, Sam walked through the house and out the door.

Moments later, he found himself standing in front of Dusty's stall in the dimly lit barn.

The horse stretched his neck over the stall door in greeting. Sam began to stroke the gelding's sturdy neck, drawing comfort from the sleek hide under his hand.

Cheryl had made it plain that she couldn't wait to get back to New York. She wouldn't stay. She didn't want him, just as Natalie hadn't wanted him.

Hurt and confusion churned inside him until he thought he might explode. Why did he keep falling for the same kind of woman? What was wrong with him?

"I won't play the fool again. I won't love her." Bold words, but Sam knew it was already too late for him.

Chapter Nine

Sam glanced with concern at his daughters seated beside him in the truck as he drove home from the hospital the next day. "You two sure are quiet."

Lindy looked at her sister and then back at him. "I don't think we have anything to say."

This didn't feel right. The doctor had given Kayla a clean bill of health, but Sam began to worry she'd been affected more than they realized. Only when they arrived home, and Kayla saw Cheryl did some of the animation return to her face.

Kayla climbed out of the truck and rushed

to Cheryl. "You're here. When you didn't come to the hospital with Daddy, I thought you might have gone away."

"I told you I'd stay until you were better."

"I'm glad you didn't leave."

Cheryl bent down and caught the child in a hug. "I'm glad you're glad." She planted a quick kiss on Kayla's cheek.

Sam's hands clenched into fists at his side. The twins adored Cheryl already. The longer she stayed, the harder it would be for them when she left. She had no right to make them love her, then leave the way their mother had.

He felt a touch on his hand, and he glanced down at Lindy's worried face. He forced a smile to his lips.

"Aren't you glad Cheryl is going to stay, Daddy?" she asked.

He met Cheryl's gaze. "Let's not forget it's only for a few more days," he answered flatly.

For a fleeting instant, he thought he saw a look of pain in Cheryl's beautiful eyes, but the expression was gone so quickly he decided he'd imagined it.

Sam expected Kayla's bubbly personality to reassert itself once she was home, but it didn't, and he watched with growing concern as she became Cheryl's little shadow. Kayla sat quietly beside Cheryl on the sofa or out on the glider when the weather was nice, but she never moved far from her new heroine's side. Lindy hovered close by, quiet and uncertain, waiting for her sister to notice her.

Two days later, he caught Cheryl's worried glance when Kayla refused to go riding with Walter. Kayla and Lindy were both good riders, and they loved to tag along on their ponies while their great-grandpa regaled them with stories of the old days. Sam spent the day with a dejected Lindy by his side, and his concerns grew. It would break Kayla's heart when Cheryl left.

That night Kayla insisted only Cheryl could tuck her in. Sam tucked Lindy in and kissed her good-night as Cheryl did the same for Kayla. They left the children's room together and climbed the stairs.

Cheryl broke the uneasy silence first. "Sam, I'm worried about Kayla."

"She's my daughter. It's my job to worry about her, not yours."

Cheryl frowned at him. "I know whose

daughter she is, but I can still see something is wrong."

"Can you? Can you see how badly Lindy feels when Kayla all but ignores her and follows you around like a puppy? Can you see how differently they act? They don't even talk the same anymore."

Cheryl laid a hand on his arm. "I see those things, but I don't see why you're angry at me."

He pulled his arm away. "Kayla turns to you now for everything, instead of her family. I think she'd get back to normal sooner if she didn't have someone interfering."

"Someone, meaning me?" Cheryl drew away from him, her voice cold and formal.

"Maybe you don't realize it, but they really care about you. Will it even matter to you that you're leaving two brokenhearted kids behind?"

"Of course I care. How can you think I don't?" When he didn't answer, she said, "I promised Kayla I would stay as long as she needed me, but if you want me to go, I will."

Sam stared at her, unable to read the expression in her eyes. He didn't want her to go. He wanted her to stay forever, but she wouldn't do that. His shoulders slumped in defeat, and he turned away feeling tired, empty and sad. "You're free to go anytime."

As the adults parted, two curly heads ducked back down the stairwell. They watched their father go out the front door while Cheryl crossed to her bedroom.

"See what you did?" Lindy hissed at her sister.

"What? I didn't do nothin'."

"Cheryl's gonna leave now."

"But I don't want her to. I want her to stay and be our mommy," Kayla insisted.

Lindy propped both elbows on her knees and rested her chin on her hands as she stared at her sister. "Are you mad at me 'cause you got hurt?"

"No."

"You never want to play anymore."

Kayla sighed. "Cheryl needs me because she's so sad. We can play tomorrow."

"Okay." With that problem solved, Lindy turned to another. "Dad's mad at Cheryl because we don't talk the same anymore," she decided at last. "Cheryl won't stay and be our mommy if Daddy's mad at her."

"So?"

"So, we got to talk the same again."

"Okay," Kayla agreed with a shrug.

"And Daddy's mad cause he thinks we'll be sad if Cheryl goes away like our real mom did."

"Then we just gotta make her stay."

"I know, but how?"

"I could hide her wallet again."

Lindy shook her head. "No, Dad would know it was us."

Kayla patted her sister's shoulder. "You'll think of something."

"Maybe. But we got to pretend we don't care if Cheryl's gonna leave, then Dad won't be mad, and they won't fight. Can you do that?"

"Sure. I can pretend better than you."

"Cannot."

"Can, too."

"Cannot."

"Last one to the bed is a monkey's uncle," Kayla cried and raced down the stairs with her sister in hot pursuit.

* * *

Free to go. I'm free to go. The phrase echoed over and over in Cheryl's mind as she lay in the darkness. If she was free to go, didn't that mean she was also free to stay?

Don't be stupid. It meant Sam wanted her to leave. And it was what she wanted, wasn't it? Yet, lying in bed, she found it impossible to imagine what her life was going to be like after she left here. It would never be the same again, of that much she was sure. Before, her heart had belonged only to dancing. Now, she was very much afraid it belonged to Sam and his children.

She stared at the ceiling. It wasn't possible, but even if she chose to stay with Sam, it would mean the end of her career. Half her life had been spent in the pursuit of one goal—to dance professional ballet. She couldn't picture her life without it. A life without grueling practices and constant pain? A life without reaching that special moment when the music swept her along like the current of a river and carried her twirling and spinning as effortlessly as a piece of driftwood. It was her gift. How could she give it up?

She turned over in the bed. Who was she kidding? She wasn't free to stay even if Sam asked her to. She was only here on borrowed time. It had been a mistake to stay in the first place. If Sam found out who she was now he wouldn't want her anywhere near his children. Maybe he was right. The sooner she left, the better off everyone would be.

The next morning, Sam and Walter sat drinking coffee in the kitchen when Cheryl came out of her room. She cast Sam a wary glance, but he avoided making eye contact. She filled a cup for herself and sat down at the table. Suddenly, the pounding of feet broke the uneasy quiet as the twins erupted from the stairwell and streaked into the kitchen. They skidded to a stop in front of their father.

"What's for—"

"—breakfast?"

"I'm—"

"—starved."

Mischievous eyes glanced at each other, and Cheryl was suddenly positive they could read each other's thoughts.

"I'm so hungry—"

"—I could eat—"

"—a cat!" they shouted together. With a fit of giggles, they darted out of the kitchen calling, "Here kitty, kitty," as they pounded down the stairs.

Sam raised an eyebrow at Cheryl, and she sputtered out a sip of coffee as she began to laugh.

"They're back," he said, giving her a sheepish smile.

Cheryl's heart lightened at the sight of that familiar lopsided grin. "Do you think we'll live to regret it?"

"Only if they catch the cat," Walter said dryly.

Cheryl giggled. "Yum, kitty catatori, my favorite."

It was good to see Sam smile again, Cheryl thought, as her traitorous heart soared.

Bonkers wisely remained out of sight until after breakfast. The twins settled for pancakes. Sam and Cheryl both watched with relief as they put away enough to feed a small army.

"Can we play outside?"

"Can Cheryl come with us to see Grandma's garden?"

"Before she goes—"

"—back to New York?"

"Maybe after lunch," Sam told them. They agreed without argument, then began to gather up the dishes and load the dishwasher without being reminded.

"We're going—"

"—to clean—"

"—our room," they announced and left the kitchen.

Sam shot Cheryl a suspicious glance. "They look like—"

"—your children, and they sound like—"

"—my children, but I wonder—"

"—whose children they really are—"

"—and what have they done with mine?"

He grinned, and Cheryl burst into laugher. "That's not as hard to do as it sounds," she said between giggles.

"All you have to do is think alike," Walter said, rising and putting his plate in the sink.

Her smile faded as she and Sam stared at each other across the kitchen table. He waited until Walter had left the room.

"Cheryl, I'm sorry about last night." He hesitated a moment, then continued, "I didn't mean the things I said. I was tired and worried. I guess I've been burning my candle at both ends trying to run the ranch and trying to prove I've still got what it takes to be an architect."

"It's all right. If I thought I would hurt the girls by staying, I'd be gone in a minute."

He nodded. "I know. I overreacted," he conceded. "They seem to understand about your leaving. I just didn't want them to get hurt again."

He stared down at the cup in his hand. "They weren't even three when their mother left, but they cried for days."

He was silent for a long time as he stared into his cup, and Cheryl saw the twins hadn't been the only ones hurt by their mother's desertion. Sam had been hurt, as well. He was still hurting, and Cheryl wanted nothing more than to ease his pain.

Reaching across the table, she touched his arm. "Do you want to talk about it?" she asked gently.

He gave a weary sigh. "I don't know where

to start. We met in college, and it was love at first sight, or so we thought. We were married before we even knew who the other person really was. My parents had always talked about their whirlwind romance, and I thought it would be the same for me."

With a sad shake of his head, he continued. "It didn't take long for the new to wear off. We should've called it quits then, but I kept thinking we could make it work."

Gazing into Cheryl's sympathetic eyes, Sam felt a lump rise in his throat. It was hard to put into words how much his wife's desertion had cost him, but he wanted her to understand.

"She hated living on the ranch. Like a fool, I believed that if she loved me enough, she'd come to love the ranch, too. When she told me she was pregnant, I was ecstatic. My mother tried to tell me Natalie wasn't happy, but I blew her off."

He shrugged. "Anyway, the twins were born eight weeks prematurely. They were in incubators the first four weeks of their life. You'd never know to look at them now, but they were so tiny it scared me to touch them.

Natalie became sick and ran a high fever after the delivery. She didn't want to see the girls. She said she was afraid she might make them sick, too. At the time, I thought she was right, so I spent every minute I could with the babies in the nursery. I knew that they needed me, needed to know that someone loved them, and I felt so bad that their mother couldn't be with them."

He moved to pour himself another cup of coffee. He hadn't been blind. For the first time, he'd admitted to himself that he'd seen all the signs of her discontent, but he had ignored them. He had been as much to blame as Natalie for the failure of their marriage.

Cheryl said, "I've seen what a good father you are. It doesn't surprise me that you spent time with them in the hospital."

"I should have spent more of that time with my wife. Anyway, once we finally got the twins home, things were better for a while, but as the girls got older, I could see Natalie was growing more and more unhappy. She said she needed to work again, so I proposed we build our own house. The money was needed to get this ranch back on its feet, but

I thought if she had a home she'd designed herself, maybe she'd be more content."

"Did it help?"

"We worked on the plans together and it was like old times for a few months. Then, after one trip she made to Kansas City, everything changed. Nothing we could get locally was good enough. She had to have special tile for the kitchen, special drapes, a dozen things that required her to travel back to KC. I never suspected she was seeing someone else.

"She filed for divorce two weeks before the girls' third birthday and gave me full custody. She said she wasn't cut out to be a mother."

"Sam, I'm so sorry."

"Now you know why I'm overprotective of them sometimes."

"I think I do."

"It took a lot of soul searching to get through that time."

Cheryl looked down and rubbed her palms on her jeans. "After I lost my mother I didn't understand how such a bad thing could happen. I was angry. Silly, wasn't it?"

"No. It was human."

Sam reached across the table. Cheryl laid her hand in his, welcoming the strength that seemed to flow from him.

"I do need your help for a bit longer. I have to be in Kansas City tomorrow. If I miss another meeting, my client will start looking for a new architect," he admitted.

"I can stay a few days longer."

But not forever, Sam thought as he studied her delicate face. And that was what he really wanted. Forever.

That afternoon, Sam announced his plan to ride out and check the pastures. "I need to see if they're dry enough to start the range burning. It's got to be done soon. The grass needs at least a month of growth before the cattle are moved out onto it. That late snow has put us behind."

While he was gone, the twins insisted Cheryl spend the afternoon with them in their grandmother's garden.

"It's the prettiest place—" Kayla began.

"—in the whole world," Lindy finished.

Cheryl agreed to go with them, but she was dismayed when she saw the path they took away from the house. Narrow and steep, it curved downward around the face of the bluff, and she eyed it with unease. Getting down it on crutches might not be a problem, but getting back up could be. The girls were already skipping down ahead of her, so she gathered her nerve and followed carefully.

The path ended at a doorway in an old stone wall. It had once been a small rock house, but as Cheryl peered through the doorway, she could see the wall with the door was the only one left standing. Tall cottonwood trees shaded the ground beyond, and Cheryl followed the twins through the opening.

Twin stone benches sat on either side of a large sundial in the middle of a shady glade surrounded by masses of nodding yellow daffodils. Hyacinths in a rainbow of colors clustered close to the paving stones around the benches and added their irresistible sweet fragrance to the air. Pointed blades of iris leaves clustered along a small stone wall that ran a dozen yards out from the corner of the old house and enclosed the glade on three sides. In one corner, the long canes of a rose bush arched in budding green sprays.

Cheryl sat down on the bench and watched the girls as they gathered flowers in the dappled shade. Their arms were loaded with early-spring blooms when they came and sat down beside her at last.

"Grandma Eleanor says this is her favorite place in the whole world," Lindy told her.

"'Cause this is where she can close her eyes and hear the sounds of happiness," Kayla added.

Both girls squeezed their eyes shut tightly and listened. Cheryl watched them with amusement. They were quiet only a few moments when Lindy shook her head. "I don't hear anything. Let's go throw rocks in the water." She took off toward the creek bank. Her bouquet lay forgotten on the bench.

"Okay," Kayla jumped up, but handed Cheryl her armload of flowers. "You listen for it. Grandma says you have to have your eyes closed."

Cheryl smiled, but she closed her eyes obediently and listened.

The warm, spring wind brushed past her cheeks like the touch of soft silk and sent the cottonwood leaves rustling overhead like the petticoats of a dozen dancers crammed into one small dressing room. Birds chirped gaily, the wind sighed through the long grass on the hillside behind her, and the sound of little voices came to her.

"I see a frog."

"Where?"

"By that log."

"Oh, I see it."

"You better go kiss him."

"Yuck! Why?"

"He might be a prince."

"I don't want a prince that bad."

"Me, neither."

"Hey, you should kiss Jimmy Slader."

"Double yuck! No way."

"Yeah, then maybe he'd turn into a frog."

Girlish giggles filled the air.

Cheryl smiled to herself. Happiness did indeed reside in the garden. The sounds of it were everywhere.

Opening her eyes, Cheryl leaned forward to study the old copper sundial aged to a deep green. She ran her finger over the raised words that circled the rim.

A time to weep,
And a time to laugh;
A time to mourn,
And a time to dance;
Eccl. 3:4

It was as if someone had written about her entire life in those four short lines.

Kayla came to sit beside Cheryl on the bench. "I like the sundial, don't you?"

"It's very pretty."

A second later, Kayla took off in pursuit of her sister.

Cheryl's fingers lingered on the worn words that rang so true to her life. "'A time for everything,'" she whispered.

Was that true? Was this a time for her with Sam and the children? If Sam hadn't been on the road that night she never would have known him or the twins. If she hadn't been beside the corral that day would Kayla be alive now? The idea that she might somehow be part of a greater design gave her pause.

The twins played until they grew sleepy in the afternoon heat, and Cheryl decided it was time to head up the hill. As they emerged from the stone doorway, Sam sat on his horse waiting for them on the other side. Cheryl's pulse jumped into double time at the sight of him.

"Afternoon ladies," he drawled and tipped his hat. "That's a mighty tall hill for a gal on crutches. Care for a lift?"

"Thank you, kind sir," she drawled in an imitation of him.

He swung down from the horse, took her crutches and laid them on the ground. She rested her arms on his shoulders as he grasped her waist and lifted her into the saddle.

His strong fingers gripping her waist sent a tingling straight down her spine. Cheryl glanced at his face as his hands lingered. What was it that she saw in those hazel eyes? She couldn't be sure because he released her abruptly and turned to swing the twins up, one in front of her and one behind her on the horse.

"Ready?" he asked.

"Yup!" the twins said.

"I think so," Cheryl answered dubiously as she looked up the steep, narrow path.

Sam picked up her crutches and handed

them to her. "Courage is its own reward, New York."

"That's virtue, cowboy."

"What's virtue?" Kayla asked.

"You explain that one," he suggested. He turned and started up the hill leading his horse.

"Thanks, cowboy. It means being very good, Kayla."

Lindy leaned around Cheryl. "Grandma wants us to be good, doesn't she, Daddy?"

"That's right."

"I'm good," Kayla declared.

"You are not," her sister stated. "You wanted to turn Jimmy Slader into a frog. That's not nice."

"Oh. I forgot that."

"You better say you're sorry."

Kayla raised her face to the heavens and called out, "I'm sorry I wanted to turn Jimmy into a frog."

What about omissions and half-truths, Cheryl wondered. Would Sam be forgiving if he ever found out?

At the front of the house, Sam stopped the horse and handed the twins down. He took the crutches from Cheryl and gave them to the girls.

Cheryl wished she could get off by herself, but before she could think of a way, his hands gripped her waist again. When her feet touched the ground, she found she couldn't move away from his touch. She avoided looking at him, afraid he would read the longing in her eyes.

He reached up to gently brush a strand of hair away from her face. "I don't know why I try to resist you," he whispered.

Her glance flew to his face. Her breath seemed to stick in her throat. He was going to kiss her. A small sound reminded her of the children staring with rapt curiosity.

"Ah, Sam," she said leaning back.

"Hmm?"

"We have an audience."

He turned his head and leveled a stern look at the twins. "Don't you two have something to do?"

Each twin held out a crutch. Cheryl reached over and took them. The girls scooted for the house.

Sam removed his hands from Cheryl's

waist with reluctance. He hated to let her go. It felt so good when she was close to him. Maybe he was playing the fool, but did he care? Just to touch her made him feel alive in a way he'd never known. He shoved his hands into his pockets. He was letting his heart rule his head. That was a sure ticket to disaster.

"I need to go to Kansas City tomorrow. Will you be okay with Walter and the girls while I'm gone?"

"I can manage without you."

He sighed and led Dusty toward the barn. "That's exactly what I'm afraid of," he told the horse.

Chapter Ten

"It's your move," Walter said as he sat across from Sam at the chess board several evenings later.

Sam tried to study the board and plan his next move, but his mind wasn't on the game. His gaze drifted to where Cheryl and the twins stood by the billiard table. She'd given in to their pleading and agreed to teach them some of the basic moves of ballet. They were using the side of the table like a dancer's barre.

"The barre is used to help you keep your balance while you practice, like so." She touched the pool table rail lightly. She wore a ballet slipper on one foot, and she rose lightly onto her toes as she held her injured foot extended in front of her.

"It's your move, Sam," Walter said again, louder this time.

"What? Oh, sure." Sam moved a dark pawn and returned to watching the dancers.

Walter's gaze traveled between Sam and Cheryl, then his lips tightened into a thin line. "I know you don't want an old man sticking his nose in your business, but you're riding for a fall with that one, Sammy. She's as out of place here as a hothouse flower."

"I don't know what you mean." He ignored Walter's snort and moved another pawn, then he glanced at the dancers once more.

She was a natural with children, Sam thought as he watched her showing them different positions. Each girl had her full attention as she gave them praise and gentle corrections. She seemed to know when they needed encouragement and when to step back and let them try on their own.

"Sam, since that was my pawn you moved,

I'm going to put it back, and we can continue this game when your mind is less occupied."

Sam pulled his attention back to Walter. "I'm sorry. What did you say?"

"I said your mind isn't on the game." The elder Hardin leaned back in his chair. "We can start burning pasture soon. The snow put us behind, but the grass should be dry enough by the first of next week."

Cheryl crossed the room and sat down with the men as the girls continued to practice. "Don't look at your feet," she called.

Walter smiled at her. "You're in for a treat, Cheryl. You can help us with pasture-burning next week."

"Not me!" She held up one hand and shot them both a look of disgust. "You go play with fire if you want to, but I'm staying right here. I have no intention of going back to New York with all the hair singed off my head."

"You'll be perfectly safe with us. Tell her, Sam."

"She can make up her own mind. Are you going to make a move or will I have to wait another six months to finish this game?"

Walter cast a speculative look between the two, then turned his attention back to the game. Cheryl rose and went back to the twins.

Sam caught a glimpse of the hurt look in her eyes before she turned away and hated himself for causing it. He was acting churlishly, and he knew it. But every time she mentioned going back to New York, he felt as if he'd taken a blow to the midsection.

He wanted her to love the ranch, to love his kids, to love him. But she already had a life she loved. A life he couldn't be a part of. She wasn't going to stay. Why couldn't he get that through his thick head? The wooden chess piece in his hand snapped in two. Sam stared at the broken queen. He rose from the table and left the room without a word.

"Where is Daddy going?"

"Doesn't he want to watch us dance?"

Cheryl's eyes followed Sam's retreating form. "I don't know where he's going."

Walter came up beside them. "I want to see you dance."

Cheryl flashed him a grateful look, and he gave her a sympathetic smile in return.

* * *

It was Walter who told Cheryl the next morning that Sam had gone to Kansas City.

"Did he say when he'd be back?" she asked, biting her lip.

"No, but he can't be gone long because there's a lot to be done here in the next few days. If he thinks I plan to work like a dog while he's off enjoying the bright lights, he's got another think coming."

Cheryl kept herself occupied and tried not to let her thoughts dwell on Sam as the days dragged by. The one good thing was that no more cryptic letters arrived for her.

To pass the time, she began helping her first students master the basic ballet positions and steps. The twins were a delight to teach. They were eager and gifted with a desire to learn, and she had discovered something new about herself in the process—she liked teaching.

"Plié means to bend," she demonstrated for the girls, "and demi-plié means a half bend, like this. Remember to do it slowly, Lindy. You don't want to look like a jack-in-the-box popping up."

"Why don't you just say *bend* if you mean bend?" Walter asked, as he lounged in a leather chair watching them. "Makes more sense. Shouldn't they be on their toes?"

"French has been the language of ballet for about four hundred years, and no they shouldn't be up on their toes. Toe dancing can't be done until a qualified teacher decides a pupil is ready for it. It's very hard on young bones."

"How old were you when you started?"

"I was very old, almost fourteen, but it was love at first sight. Once I'd seen a ballet, I never wanted to do anything else. It wasn't easy to start training at that age, but I was lucky. My cousin knew a wonderful dancing master who took me on as a private pupil. I had a natural flexibility and lots of determination. It's much better if a child starts learning at age six or seven."

"It won't do Lindy and Kayla any good to start this young," Walter said, standing up.

"Why do you say that?" She frowned at him.

"Who'll teach them after you're gone?"

Cheryl didn't have an answer, and some of

the joy she felt went out of the day. The girls were so eager to learn. Surely they would be able to continue.

"There must be a dance school in town?"

"I don't think so," Walter scoffed.

"Maybe not in Council Grove or Strong City, but in Manhattan they must have some."

"An hour's drive from here? I doubt Sam will want to take them that far for dancing lessons."

"You think dance lessons would be a waste of time, don't you?" she asked, amazed at his attitude even though she knew she shouldn't be.

He shrugged, but didn't answer. He didn't have to. She read the answer on his face, and her temper flared. "If it doesn't teach them to cook, mend fences or haggle a better price out of some cattle buyer, it's a waste of time, right?"

She planted her hands on her hips. "You've been past the cattle crossing at Bazaar. You know the world is a lot bigger than this ranch, and these children deserve the chance to discover for themselves where their heart's desire lies."

Walter's eyes narrowed, and he watched her silently for a long moment. "There's something about you that doesn't add up."

Taken aback, she stiffened. "I don't know what you mean."

"For one thing, you know a lot more about ranching than you let on. And when you're mad, that New York accent fades faster than the flavor of penny bubble gum. Who are you?"

Cheryl stared at him, her mind racing. She'd gotten careless again. Her gaze fell before the suspicion in his eyes. "I'm nobody special. But I do care about the twins, and about Sam."

"Do you?"

Her gaze snapped back to his. "Yes," she answered firmly.

His gaze grew stern. "Then maybe you shouldn't tempt them with things they can't have."

They stared at each other silently. He wasn't talking about dance lessons, and she knew it. Jamming his hat on his head, he left the room, and she chewed her lip as she watched him walk away. Was that what she'd been doing?

Tempting Sam, and herself, with something they couldn't have?

Maybe Walter was right. She didn't have a reason to stay now. She had her wallet back, and she could tag along with her company once she caught up with them. Kayla was fully recovered.

Only, she didn't want to leave. She wanted to be a part of this family. She'd never felt so torn in her entire life.

She missed Sam, Cheryl realized as she turned her attention back to the girls and corrected Kayla's foot position. She missed his boyish grin and hearty laughter. She missed the amused glances they shared when the twins provided some unintentional humor. She missed him a lot. If it was like this after he'd been gone only two days, what would it be like when she left for good?

Sam showed up in the kitchen for breakfast the next day. He wore an enormous grin on his face. The twins raced to hug him and he scooped them both up before stopping in front of Cheryl. "They bought my design."

"For the house in Kansas City?" she asked.

"Yup."

"Oh, Sam, I'm so glad."

"You and me both. We start construction in two weeks. And we're gonna burn pasture today," he announced, twirling around once with the girls in his arms.

"Cheryl, you got to—"

"—come and watch," the twins told her.

"I will be able to see it from here. That's close enough," she assured them.

"Girls, leave Cheryl alone. If she's too chicken to come and set the world on fire, then she should stay home."

"Chicken? Who are you calling a chicken, cowboy?" she demanded.

"Hey, if the feather fits…" He put the girls down, folded his arms and flapped his elbows like wings. "Chicken!"

"Chicken! Chicken!" The twins took up the chant.

"Come on, it'll be fun," Sam coaxed.

He grinned when she folded her arms across her chest, raised one eyebrow and looked at him in disbelief.

"Please come, Cheryl," the twins begged. "Please."

"All right. But only to prove to your father that I'm not a chicken."

An hour later, she sat in Sam's pickup and rested her arms on the open window as she watched the activity going on around her. She'd seen the huge fires when she was a child, but she'd never helped set them. Three trucks lined up along the fence inside an immense pasture. A plump, elderly woman wearing a pink shirt and faded jeans tucked into cowboy boots stood handing out donuts and coffee to the men as they grouped around the tailgate of one truck. Sam took her elbow and separated her from the cowhands. He led her over to the truck where Cheryl sat.

Cheryl was thankful for the wide round sunglasses that hid her eyes. Sam stopped beside her.

"Cheryl, this is Mrs. Webster. It's her pasture we're burning today."

"And I can't thank you enough for doing this, Sam," Mrs. Webster said. "With my Simon laid up after his heart surgery I never would have gotten this work done."

"It's my pleasure."

"I'd better be getting back to the house. Simon gets fit to be tied if I'm gone long. I wish I could pay you with more than coffee and donuts."

Sam slipped an arm around her ample shoulders. "Your donuts are worth their weight in gold, Mrs. Webster, and that's a fact."

"Still, it don't seem right, you and your crew doing this for nothing."

"You would do the same for us if the shoe was on the other foot. In fact, when Dad passed away, you and Simon were the first ones to come with food and offers of help."

"I'm lucky to have such good people for friends and neighbors. How is your sister doing? I heard your mother went to Denver to stay with her."

Sam winked at Cheryl. "It's hard to keep a secret in a small town, isn't it?"

Cheryl swallowed hard and hoped her guilt didn't show on her face.

Sam didn't seem to notice. "Becky has been in and out of the hospital twice with early labor. Mom is staying to help out. We miss her, but we know Becky needs her at a time like this."

"I'll keep you and all your family in my thoughts and prayers, Samuel. It's the least I can do to repay all you've done for me and mine." She wiped her eye with her sleeve, then hurried away.

Cheryl studied Sam's face. "You like helping people, don't you?"

His smile lightened her heart. "Do unto others. That's the way I was taught to live."

Her father would have finished the quote with *before they do it to you.*

Sam wasn't like the ranchers her father had badmouthed and stolen from. Only, maybe those ranchers had been good men, too. She once told Angie that she didn't regret anything she had done in the past. It seemed that was no longer true. Not if she had hurt people like Sam or Walter or Mrs. Webster.

Shaking off her deep thoughts, she pointed to the men waiting to get started. "Tell me about this job. Why three trucks?"

He explained, "The first truck lights the grass afire from a torch pulled along behind it. The second truck is equipped with a pressurized water sprayer, and it puts out the blaze as it follows alongside the torch. The third truck follows the others putting out any little fires that are missed. This way we create a burn line that will contain the main fire."

"You backfire the whole pasture that way?"

He gave her a look of surprise. "That's right. Once we get a strip done around the entire perimeter, we'll fire the grass inside and let the wind push the blaze across the range. When the fire reaches the strip on the other side that's already burnt, it dies out from lack of fuel."

"You do this every year?"

"Some ranchers do. I prefer a three-year rotation because it gives the wildlife a break. Prairie chickens, for instance, prefer newly burned pasture for feeding and mating. They like to nest in the two-year-old grass, but they prefer to seek cover in the thicker grass that's three years old or older."

Cheryl shot him a skeptical look. "How do you know what a prairie chicken prefers?"

Sam pushed the brim of his hat up with one finger and grinned. "Well, ma'am, I asked them."

She tried, but couldn't smother a chuckle.

Walter came to stand beside Sam. "I think we're ready."

Both men moved away to talk with the rest of the crew.

Cheryl pulled her sunglasses off and looked for the twins. They were busy gathering long branches of snowy blossoms from a thicket of wild sand plums growing along the pasture fence.

After a detailed check of all his equipment, Sam ordered the burning started. He watched as the sprayer truck followed closely behind Walter, then he headed back toward his pickup and called to the twins. A small gust of wind crossed the freshly burned strip and carried a flurry of ashes toward the truck.

Cheryl pulled back from the window and gave a cry of pain as she covered one eye with her hand.

Sam was beside her in an instant. "What's the matter?"

"Something blew in my eye."

"Don't rub it. Let me see." He opened the truck door, jerked off his gloves and bent close. With gentle fingers, he removed a cinder from the corner of her eye.

Cheryl blinked rapidly. "Thanks, cowboy."

"You're welcome, New York," he replied softly. His gaze was drawn to her tempting lips. Ever so slowly, he bent toward her.

"Cheryl, look at—"

"—all the flowers we found."

The twins squirmed in between them and held up grubby hands filled with flowers and clumps of clinging dirt. Sam drew back.

"They're beautiful, girls," Cheryl said, taking the offered bouquet. "These wild plums smell wonderful, don't they? But I'm afraid this old milkweed will make me sneeze."

Sam frowned. "I didn't think they had milkweed in New England. It's a prairie plant."

Cheryl's gaze shot to his, and her eyes widened. Suddenly, she smacked the flowers into his chest, and he jumped. "What on earth?"

"Bee! Sam, there's a bee on you. I'll get it." She hit him again, spreading dirt and petals across his shirt.

The twins watched with puzzled faces. Lindy said, "I don't see a bee."

"Me, neither," Kayla added.

"It's gone now." Cheryl dropped the tattered remains of her bouquet and put her sunglasses on. "Don't you think we had better catch up with the others, Sam? Come on, girls, get in the truck."

Sam brushed the dirt from his shirt as he walked around to the driver's side. What had that been all about? He didn't have time to ponder the question. The other trucks were pulling ahead of them.

The twins climbed in with Cheryl. They both wanted to sit beside her, and she forestalled an argument by lifting Kayla over her lap and placing one child on each side. She looked at Sam as he got behind the wheel, and he gave her a rueful grin.

"Can we—" Lindy started.

"—see the fire?" Kayla asked.

"Will it make—"

"—lots of smoke?"

"What makes the smoke go up?"

"Where does it go after it goes up?"

Sam said, "Remind me to leave them at home next time."

Cheryl grinned at him. "I would have had to stay at home with them."

"You're right. Remind me to let them ride with Walter."

"Now that's a good idea, cowboy."

By late afternoon, the thrill had worn off for the twins, and Sam looked over to see both girls asleep as they leaned on Cheryl. Even Cheryl's head was nodding as he followed slowly behind the others, occasionally stopping to put out a small fire the main water truck had missed. It was boring work, but the entire pasture perimeter had to be backfired carefully before the main fires could be lit.

The trucks were nearly back at the starting point when a movement off to his right caught Sam's attention. A white-tailed doe sprang out of a brushy ravine as the wind carried the smoke in her direction. Sam watched as she bounded back into cover only to reappear a moment later. Nervously, she watched the trucks and stamped her front leg in a signal of alarm. After a moment, she bounded back down the ravine.

She's got a fawn down there, Sam thought, slowing his truck. He glanced at Cheryl and the girls. The twins dozed quietly, and only Cheryl's eyes opened when the truck stopped.

"Are we done?" she asked, trying to stifle a yawn.

"We're back where we started from, but we're a long way from done." He smiled as she gave a sleepy nod and closed her eyes again.

"I'll be back in a minute," he said, stepping out of the truck. He didn't want Cheryl or the girls to know about the deer. Area wildlife would head for the creeks and ponds when the grass started burning, but a newborn fawn wouldn't stand much of a chance. He decided to check the ravine and see if the doe had hidden a baby too young to run.

Cheryl heard Sam leave the truck. She opened her eyes long enough to see him start toward a deep gully that cut between two loaf-shaped hills. She sat up and rubbed her eyes. The twins slept soundly as they leaned against her.

Several minutes had passed when the radio crackled, and Walter's voice came over the speaker. "The wind is gusting a bit harder now, Sam. I'm going to get started."

It was a moment before her sleepy brain processed the fact that Walter's truck had turned and was coming back toward them. He had set fire to the grass inside the burnt strip, and the breeze was already pushing the flames out across the prairie.

She grabbed the mike and fumbled with it an instant before she was able to call out, "Walter, stop! Sam went down into that ravine."

His truck veered off the grass and stopped.

His voice barked over the radio to the other truck. "Get the sprayer going and put this out. Sam's in front of the fire!"

Cheryl saw the men on the second truck scrambling to get the water sprayer started again. The wind kicked up in a sudden brisk gust, and the fire gained momentum, crackling and snapping as the flames swept through the tall, dry grass.

Walter jumped out of his truck and began running toward the gully, yelling Sam's name. Thick gray-white smoke rose in a dense curtain from the flames and obscured everything beyond it. A swirling column of hot air sprang up in the blazing grass, and a spark-laden whirlwind danced ahead of Walter spreading the fire even faster. He threw his arms in front of his face and backed away as a wall of flames flared in front of him. He was still shouting Sam's name.

Sam walked down the ravine slowly scanning the underbrush for the white dotted pattern of a fawn's back. A rustling in the brush ahead of him and the flash of a white tail bounding away gave him a clue, but he nearly stepped on the little thing before he saw it.

"Your mama did a good job of hiding you, didn't she?" he spoke softly as he knelt down beside the huddled fawn.

He gathered the quivering infant into his arms. "You can't be more than a few hours old. It's just your bad luck to be born so early in the spring. Someone forgot to tell your mama you weren't supposed to be born for another month. Let's get you out of harm's way, shall we?"

He looked into its liquid brown eyes and

sighed. "Those girls of mine will want to keep you. I can just see it. In a year's time, I'll have a six-point buck in the house with a big red bow around his neck. I hope you like cats."

Sam heard Walter calling him as he made his way back up the steep ravine. Suddenly, the crackling of fire drowned out Walter's voice. Smoke swirled down into the draw, and the fawn began to struggle in his arms.

Sam spun around and sprinted down the gully away from the fire. Of all the witless blunders he had pulled in his life, this was the stupidest. He'd walked off without telling Walter, and he'd assumed the men in the other trucks had seen him. It was a careless mistake that might cost him his life.

He knew a small creek curved across the prairie a quarter of a mile from the base of these hills. It was a slim chance but it was all he had. To make it, he'd have to run the race of his life. He wasn't going to die without a fight—his girls needed him. He glanced down at the tiny deer. If he was going to have any chance, he knew he'd have to leave the fawn behind.

* * *

Cheryl watched as Walter backed away from the blaze. She stared in stunned disbelief as the fire engulfed the ravine Sam had entered. Her mind recoiled in horror as the flames shot higher when they reached the thick brush that grew there.

A moan escaped her lips, and she swayed in the seat. The radio mike dropped from her nerveless fingers. She clapped her hands over her own mouth to keep from screaming. Tearing her gaze away from the fire, she looked down at the twins. They continued to sleep quietly on either side of her. *Please don't let them wake up and see this.*

The men on the water truck fought a losing battle as the fire spread out in front of them. One man jumped from the truck and ran to pull Walter away from the fire's edge. Walter shook him off and staggered back to his pickup. He braced both arms on the hood and bowed his head. After a long moment, he walked to the open truck door, leaned in and grabbed the radio mike. Cheryl didn't hear any sound from her set. He'd turned the radio to the emergency channel, she realized, and he was calling for help. He dropped his head onto his arms when he finished and leaned on the truck door as if it were the only thing in the world that could hold him up.

The other cowboy took the mike from him and laid a hand on his shoulder. Walter straightened and looked toward Cheryl. He began to walk slowly toward her.

At the bottom of the ravine, Sam paused and looked back. The flames were gaining on him. Upward and to his left, he saw the hill ended in a rocky outcropping. The crumbling limestone cliff was free of brush, and a shelf of stone jutted out like a small cave. It was a better gamble than the creek, and he scrambled upward with the fawn still cradled in his arms.

He stretched out under the low rock shelf and hoped he didn't find himself sharing it with a copperhead. It would be just his luck to survive the fire and die of snakebite. The fawn squirmed in his arms, but he held it tightly as the fire swept around the hill below them. Thick smoke choked him, and he pulled his bandanna up to cover his nose and mouth.

A picture of Cheryl with her arms full of

plum blossoms flashed into his mind. He regretted now he hadn't kissed her at the truck. If he were going to die, he'd much rather die with the memory of her sweet kiss still on his lips.

He huddled under the rock ledge as burning embers fell beside him from the hilltop's grassy overhang. Heavy smoke billowed around him; the heat became intense as the fire devoured the heavy brush at the foot of the cliff a few feet below him. The fawn stopped struggling, and he wondered if it had passed out from the smoke. He sheltered its small body as best he could.

Walter stopped at the open window beside Cheryl. She saw the agony in his ancient eyes, and her heart trembled.

"It's good that they're asleep. They shouldn't see this," he said when he saw the girls on the seat beside her.

"Sam?" she whispered.

"He's got a chance. There's a creek a little ways below these bluffs." From the look in his eyes, Cheryl knew the chance wasn't a good one.

"I want you to take the girls home and wait for us."

"No! Walter, don't make me leave. I can't."

His lips thinned in a tight grimace of pain, and she read the determination in his face. "Sam wouldn't want his children here no matter what happens, and you know it."

She glanced at the twins and nodded in resignation. "Yes, you're right."

She had to take care of Sam's children even if her soul screamed out the need to stay.

As one of the young cowboys drove them back toward the ranch, Cheryl turned in her seat and looked through the rear window. Towering columns of smoke obscured the hills as the line of orange flames raced across the prairie leaving behind only flat, black ash smoldering with a thousand tiny plumes of white smoke. The other cowboys gathered beside Walter. It was a grim-faced group of men who stood together and waited for the fire to sweep past the base of the hills before they began their grisly search.

Chapter Eleven

"Where's Daddy?"

Cheryl turned away from the balcony door to see Kayla and Lindy standing in the middle of the room. Sirens sounded in the distance, and she slid the door closed against the eerie wailing. "He's still out at the pasture with Grandpa Walter."

Cheryl tried to keep the twins occupied, but she couldn't keep her eyes off the clock. Sam had to be all right. He was a strong man, he could have outrun the fire and made it to safety. Any minute now, he would come through the door and tell some exciting tale about sharing the creek with catfish and rabbits. Any minute now.

The minutes became an hour, then two, and still no word. She refused to give in to the despair that threatened her. She couldn't accept that she would never see him again. Her nerves were stretched to the breaking point when she heard the sound of a car pulling into the driveway, and she hurried to the open front door.

It wasn't Sam or even Walter who got out of the car in the drive, it was Merci Slader.

She didn't try to hide her dislike of Cheryl. "I was on my way home and Sam asked me to come by and tell you and the girls that he's okay."

"He's safe?" The welcome fact penetrated Cheryl's mind, and her knees nearly buckled with relief.

"He has a few scrapes and bruises and some mild smoke inhalation, but when I left the hospital, he was getting cleaned up and ready to leave. They were able to save the fawn, but the vet wants to keep it a few more days."

Cheryl stared at her in confusion. "What fawn?"

Merci walked past Cheryl into the house. "I'll let Sam tell you that story. I still can't believe he risked his life to save a stupid deer."

The twins came racing up the stairs, then stopped short. "Hi, Mrs. Slader," Kayla said.

"Hello, girls. I have a treat for you. How would you like to come and spend the night at my house? Your dad thought it was a great idea."

"I guess." They cast each other a dubious glance.

She bent toward them. "We're going to have pizza and go to a movie. Doesn't that sound like fun?"

The girls looked at Cheryl. She smiled and nodded. "A movie sounds like lots of fun. It was very nice of Mrs. Slader to offer. Go get your pj's and toothbrushes."

The twins went back downstairs without arguing, and Merci turned to Cheryl. "I thought Sam might need some time to recover from his ordeal. Obviously, he's going to need some rest and quiet. I know he can't get that with those girls in the house. I mean, I'm sure you do your best, but they do need a firm hand."

"Are you sure Sam is all right?"

Merci studied her closely. "I'm sure."

Cheryl knew her relief must be plastered across her face. She only hoped her love for Sam wasn't plain to see, as well.

Sam saw Cheryl standing out on the balcony when he came in later that evening. He watched her for a long moment through the windows. She stood with her arms clasped tightly across her middle as she faced the night. Beyond her, the southern sky glowed with the eerie orange light of prairie fires.

A soft south wind carried the faint scent of smoke drifting to him through the open sliding glass door. The same breeze fluttered the edges of her blue skirt and toyed with her loose hair. Her pale curls seemed to reach out and beckon him.

"It does look as if the whole world is on fire." She spoke without turning.

"It's a long way off. You don't have to worry about it coming this way," he said, moving to stand behind her. Her scent filled his nostrils and stirred a fierce longing to hold her in his arms once more. He closed his eyes and bowed his head. He was tired of fighting this attraction to her.

He placed his hands gently on her shoulders and pulled her against his chest. She leaned back with a sigh as he folded his arms around her and rested his cheek against the softness of her hair. The silky strands caressed his face as the breeze stirred them. He didn't want to let her go, not tonight, not ever.

"Oh, Sam, I was so frightened." Her voice trembled.

"Hush, don't talk. Just let me hold you," he whispered. For a long time they stood together and watched the distant hills burning brightly in the night.

Cheryl welcomed Sam's warmth and strength. She needed to be held in his arms. She needed to feel that he was real and whole. After a time, she turned in his arms. "I hoped you would come back to me safe and sound."

"And I hoped for a chance to do this." He lowered his head and captured her lips in a sweet and thrilling kiss that sent her heart flying with happiness.

When they drew apart at last, Cheryl looked up into his eyes. They glittered with reflected starlight. She had never felt like this about anyone before in her life. The power of the emotions he stirred scared her to death.

She drew away from him unsure of what to say. In spite of how she felt, she knew any relationship between them was doomed. She didn't want to hurt him. Not ever.

No, what she wanted was to throw herself back in his arms and hang on to the first good thing that had come into her life in a long time. But staying here would mean facing her past, her grandmother and the community that once shunned her.

"I'm sorry," Sam said, dropping his arms to his sides. "Maybe the kiss was out of line, but I don't regret it. I care for you a great deal."

It was so much more than she deserved.

He spoke again quickly. "It won't happen again. I hope this doesn't drive you away."

"No, of course not." Because she wanted to be near him for whatever time she had left. "I know you need help watching the girls. I'll stay another week, but I can't promise more. My sister will be home from her honeymoon then. After that, I'll be going to stay with her."

It was late the next morning when Sam woke. He stretched stiff, sore muscles that creaked in protest after a day of fire fighting. After dressing, he left the bedroom and saw Cheryl out on the balcony, cradling a steaming cup in her hands as she leaned a hip against the railing. She was dressed in a pair of jeans and a yellow shirt. Her hair was pulled back in a long ponytail, and her shoulders were slumped. It struck him that she looked more like a lonely kid than an elegant dancer.

She turned around at the sound of the sliding glass door opening and smiled. He smiled back, but wondered why she often seemed so sad when she thought no one was looking. "'Morning."

"'Morning? It's almost noon, lazy bones. Walter left to check the fence in the west pasture an hour ago. He told me to tell you to feed the horses."

"Okay. Come on, I could use some help."

"Doing what?"

"Someone has to explain to Dusty why his breakfast is late."

Cheryl followed Sam out to the barn, happy to be included in his day. She drank in the sight of him as he worked. He lifted the heavy bales of hay effortlessly as the muscles of his broad back and shoulders bunched and flexed beneath his faded denim shirt. She was leaning against the barn stall when she felt a nudge at her back and turned to find Dusty looking for some attention.

Sam finished his chores and came to stand beside her as she patted the horse's neck. "Want to see something cute?"

"Another new calf?"

"Think smaller, but kind of hard to get to."

"What and where?"

"I can't tell you what, but where is in the hayloft."

She pointed to her cast. "Sam, I can't climb up there."

"Sure you can. Do you trust me?"

"Maybe."

"Yes or no?"

"I think so. Why?"

"Good." He grabbed her and hefted her over his shoulder.

"What are you doing?" she shrieked. "Put me down!" She pummeled his back as he strode to the front of the barn.

"You can't climb the hayloft ladder with that cast on, New York. I'm helping you up."

"Oh, no you don't! You are *not* going to carry me up a ladder like this!"

"Relax. You don't weigh any more than a flea. I've carried sacks of grain up there that were bigger than you."

"Oh, that's great. How many of them have you dropped?"

"Not more than five or six. Hey, grab that horse blanket."

"Why should I?"

"The hay is soft, but it's prickly. Take my advice and grab the blanket."

Cheryl snatched the dark blue blanket off the stall door as he walked past. At least if he dropped her, she'd have something to break her fall.

He quickly started up the wooden ladder beside the front door. With a squeak, Cheryl squeezed her eyes shut and grabbed on to his belt as the barn floor dropped away beneath her.

"Okay, you can let go now," Sam said as he stepped onto the solid floor and set her down.

She glared at him. "That was not fun, Sam!"

He grinned. "Yes, it was."

"Look, you big, bullheaded cowboy. If you think for one minute that I enjoyed that…!"

He touched his finger to his lips. "Hush."

"I will not be hushed."

"You'll wake the babies."

She scowled at him. "What babies?"

He walked to a stack of bales, dropped to his belly in the hay and motioned for her to do the same. "Come see."

Cheryl lay on the hay beside him and looked into a space between the hay bales. A small gray cat looked back at her with luminous green eyes. Beside her, four long-haired, yellow, newborn kittens slept nestled together.

Sam grinned at Cheryl. "I found them yesterday morning. I think Bonkers is a father."

Her giggle was music to his ears. A lifetime

with this woman wouldn't be enough. His grin faded, and he sobered at the thought. What if she didn't stay? What if all he had wasn't enough for her?

The days that followed were some of the happiest Cheryl could remember. One afternoon, Sam installed a long wooden barre and a full-length mirror on the rec-room wall. Delighted, Cheryl spent hours practicing and teaching the twins to use it properly. While Sam and Walter finished burning the range, Cheryl took care of the house and the children. She dusted off her cooking skills and beamed with pride when Sam complimented her meals.

Sitting at the table in the evenings, she listened to Sam and Walter discuss the ranch work and their breeding programs. It was strange and yet wonderful to feel so included in the lives of the people she'd grown to love. Was this what belonging to a family was supposed to feel like?

The next afternoon, the twins persuaded her to help them fly their kites, and she followed them across to the hillside opposite the house. As they passed the old oak tree, she saw that someone had nailed wooden strips to its slanted trunk, and a few planks were visible in its leafy branches.

"Is this your tree house?" Cheryl asked as she sat down in the shade. Bonkers climbed into her lap for attention.

"It was Daddy's and Aunt Becky's."

"When they were little like us."

"I see." Cheryl smiled as she imagined a young Sam, the budding architect, constructing it.

The twins ran to launch their kites, and the western breeze carried them quickly out over the valley below the hillside. Cheryl leaned back against the trunk of the tree and watched as the red-and-yellow kites dipped and soared in the wind silhouetted against the blue sky and the fluffy white clouds that drifted by. She closed her eyes and took a deep breath of fresh air on a glorious spring day.

A meadowlark sang somewhere in the tall grass, and the wind stirred the branches overhead and set them to whispering. The children laughed and shouted, and on her lap Bonkers purred in contentment.

"A penny for your thoughts," a voice spoke above her.

She opened one eye and squinted up at Sam as he towered over her. He tipped the brim of his hat up and leaned his broad shoulder against the tree trunk. "Or aren't they worth that much?"

"I was just thinking how brave your parents were."

His brow wrinkled. "What do you mean?"

"To spend all that money to send you to college to study architecture after they saw your early work." She pointed above them.

He glanced up at the haphazard tree house. "You might not believe it, but I had a beautiful set of blueprints to follow. That was when I discovered an architect is only as good as his builder. I also discovered I was much better with paper than with a hammer and nails." He sat down beside her. "Mind if I share your tree?"

"Not at all, just promise me you won't haul me up to see your tree house first-hand." Cheryl could have bitten her wayward tongue as a speculative gleam leapt into Sam's eyes.

He studied the boards above them but slowly shook his head.

"It's an idea, but I don't think those old timbers could take the stress," he said as he grinned at her.

She shot him a look of disgust. "Don't you have some ranch work to do?"

He leaned close and whispered in her ear, "I do, but I'd rather spend the time with you. Unfortunately, I'm needed in one of the pastures. I just stopped to tell you that Gramps and I'll be in late for supper." He rose and tipped his hat in her direction, then strode away.

She sat up straight and gave her attention to the children while trying to ignore the happy hum of her pulse.

As much as Cheryl liked the girls, watching two active and imaginative kids turned out to be harder than she believed possible.

Sam came into the house the next afternoon as she was cleaning up, followed by two contrite-looking children. Cheryl stared at them in surprise. She'd thought they were downstairs watching TV. In fact, she could still hear the sounds of cartoons coming up the stairwell.

His tone was stern as he crossed his arms and said, "Show Cheryl what you did."

Lindy glanced once at his set face then held out her hands. Messy globs of vibrant pink covered her fingertips as she held out an empty bottle of nail polish. Cheryl took the vial and looked to Sam for an explanation. She'd used her favorite shade of Rose Petal Pink just that morning, and she was sure she'd left the bottle on the dresser in her room.

"Apologize for taking something that didn't belong to you," Sam said.

Kayla's face was downcast. "We're sorry."

"We just wanted to—"

"—look as pretty—"

"—as you do." They fell silent and stared at their feet.

"Tell her the rest," Sam said sternly.

"Let me guess," Cheryl said, looking at Sam. "Bonkers is now pink?"

"No, but not because they didn't try."

"He wouldn't hold still," Lindy said, looking contrite.

"Harvey held still," Sam told her. "My prize breeding bull has hot pink hooves."

While Cheryl had learned that Harvey really was a gentle giant, she blanched at the thought of these two crawling into his pen and painting his feet. He could have trampled them without even trying. "Sam, I'm so sorry. I thought they were downstairs, honest."

"They're going to be—in their room until supper time and no TV tonight. Is that understood?"

"Yes, Daddy," they agreed together, and left the room.

When they were out of earshot, Cheryl burst into laughter. "A bull with pink toenails. This I've got to go see."

Sam shook his head, but he was grinning, too. "I plan on moving him into the Hazy Creek pasture with four new cows on Saturday. I just hope the heifers don't get jealous. Buying nail polish for the entire herd could bankrupt me."

"I'm out of pink, but I've got some red you can borrow if that will help keep the peace."

Sam chuckled. "No, thanks. I came in to tell you that Walter's going into Council

Grove tomorrow. If you want, you and the twins can ride along. Kayla says her boots are pinching her toes. Do you think you can help her find some new ones? I would take her, but I've got another meeting with my firm."

Cheryl hesitated. Each time she went to town, she was courting disaster. What if someone recognized her?

Sam noticed her hesitation. "Forget I mentioned it. I can't keep adding more and more to your duties."

How could she deny him anything? In truth, she didn't want to. "I think a temporary ninny should be able to manage a new pair of shoes."

"Thanks. And I mean for everything you do."

Cheryl held the memory of his warm gaze close to her heart all day long.

Finding a new pair of boots in town Friday afternoon turned out to be easy enough. Cheryl and the girls finished their shopping a full half hour before the time Walter had agreed to pick them up.

"What shall we do now?" Cheryl asked.

"We could get some ice cream," Lindy suggested.

"That sounds good," Cheryl agreed.

She began walking toward the river that divided the town. The girls skipped along beside her, chattering happily. They crossed the bridge, and Cheryl saw the town had added a new statue on the east bank as she passed a larger-than-life bronze figure of a Kaw Indian warrior. Across the street stood the monument of the Madonna of the Plains, a pioneer woman looking westward with her children at her side. The small Kansas town was fiercely proud of its place in the history of the West.

The bright red ice-cream shop stood sandwiched between the street and the sloping bank of the river. Once they had their cones, the girls ran back to play around the Indian statue, and Cheryl followed along behind them. She was admiring the artist's work when the sound of squealing tires pierced the stillness. She looked up to see a battered green-and-white pickup swerving to miss a car that had stopped to turn. The pickup accelerated and sped out of town.

Cheryl watched with a sense of unease as the weaving green-and-white truck disappeared down the highway. She turned to the girls. "We told Walter we'd meet him in front of the shoe store. We'd better hurry."

The twins eagerly displayed their new boots for Walter, but Cheryl herded the girls into his truck and quickly climbed in after them, happy to be heading back to the seclusion of the ranch.

Monday morning Kayla came into the kitchen and laid several envelopes on the counter. "Is there anything for us? Grandma said she'd write to us."

"Let me see." Cheryl picked up the mail and sorted through it until she discovered a white envelope with her name on it. It didn't have a return address or a postmark, she noted. Someone must have left it in the mailbox.

"Nothing for you," she told the girls. When they left the room, she tore open the letter, pulled out a single sheet of paper, and stared at the message. In block letters in the middle of the page were the words,

LEAVE NOW!

Chapter Twelve

Who could have written the ominous note and why? Cheryl continued to puzzle over the question two days later while she waited for Dr. Carlton to finish examining her foot. Merci Slader was the obvious choice, but she didn't seem to have trouble voicing her sentiments in person, so why the cryptic nature of the note? The other possibility was that someone had recognized her. Someone who didn't want to confront her face-to-face.

"Your fractures are healing well," Dr. Carlton's voice interrupted her thoughts. "I think we can trade in this cast for a heavy splint if you promise to take it easy."

Cheryl agreed and waited impatiently as he cut through the thick plaster. The footgear he replaced it with reminded her of a cumbersome ski boot.

When he was finished, the doctor scribbled a note on her chart, then paused and peered at her over the edge of his glasses. "How's Sam feeling?" he asked.

"Fine." She couldn't help the foolish grin that spread across her face.

"That's good," Dr. Carlton muttered absently.

A light tap sounded on the door, and Merci opened it. "Doctor, you have a call holding." She ignored Cheryl completely.

Cheryl stood and tested her balance on the new splint.

"Thank you, Merci," he said. "If you'll wait a second, I'll be done with this chart. Ms. Steele, these are your instructions for care of this splint. Oh, by the way," he said, glancing at Cheryl, "I solved the mystery of why I thought I'd met you before."

"You did?" Cold prickles of fear crept down Cheryl's spine.

"Yes, you bear a striking resemblance to a patient I had—oh—it must have been about fifteen years ago." He continued writing on her chart. "Such a beautiful, sad woman. I only saw her once."

"And you remember her after all this time?" Merci asked.

"Yes. She came in with a broken wrist. From the type of fracture and other bruises, and after meeting her husband, I suspected that he might have done it. I never found out for sure. She died tragically in a car accident right after she left my office."

Cheryl felt the blood drain from her face, and she groped behind her for the exam table.

"Her name was Mira Thatcher," he added, snapping the chart shut. "I don't suppose you could be related? The resemblance is remarkable."

Cheryl gripped the edge of the table. He'd known her mother. He must have been one of the last people to see her alive. Dozens of questions poured through her mind. She wanted to ask him about everything that had happened that day. She looked up and met Merci's speculative stare across the room.

"You mean that thieving Thatcher bunch?" Merci asked with a sneer, taking the chart he handed her.

Cheryl turned and reached, with a hand that wasn't quite steady, for her purse on the chair against the wall.

Dr. Carlton said, "They're not exactly the sort of relatives one would want to claim. They're rather infamous, locally. Doris Thatcher still lives on the family ranch."

"And you know she isn't playing with a full deck," Merci said. "She's in this office every other week with some new complaint. The woman is a hypochondriac."

"Merci," the doctor chided. "We can't talk about our patients in front of others. You know that."

"Well, the whole family is a bunch of no-good thieves."

The doctor scowled at her over the rim of his glasses. "They aren't exactly the James Gang."

"Close enough. Even the kids helped the old man steal cattle. My dad's cousin was one of the deputies that arrested them. He said Hank and his son gave up easy enough, but the older girl lit out of the barn on a big, black horse before anyone could stop her. She ran down one of the deputies and nearly killed him. They chased her across country for more than five miles before her horse gave out."

"What happened to them?" Cheryl asked, desperate to know if her whereabouts was common knowledge.

Dr. Carlton stroked his chin with one hand. "The father and son went to prison. I believe Hank died there. Liver cancer, if I remember right. The son got out about a year ago."

Merci nodded. "He lives out with the old woman. Cattle still disappear around here. We know who's responsible, but the sheriff says he can't prove it. One of these days, Thatcher will slip up and go straight back to prison where he belongs."

The doctor stuffed his pen in his pocket. "I don't know what happened to the girls. Doris never mentions them."

Merci's eyes narrowed. "Are you okay, Ms. Steele? You look a bit pale."

Cheryl forced a smile to her stiff lips. "I'm fine. At least you didn't hang them. Isn't that what they do to—what's the term?"

"Rustlers," Dr. Carlton supplied.

"Ah, yes." Cheryl nodded.

He chuckled. "We don't hang horse thieves or rustlers anymore, Miss Steele. Kansas has modern law enforcement, just like they do in New York."

"Of course. I guess I've seen one too many movies." Cheryl felt tiny droplets of sweat forming on her forehead. The air seemed thick and heavy, making it hard to breathe. She fought to remain calm. No one had forgotten or forgiven her and her family. She had been so foolish to stay.

She left the doctor's office and crossed the parking lot to the pickup Sam had loaned her for the day just as Merci Slader caught up with her. "Ms. Steele, you forgot your instructions."

Cheryl took the paper Merci held out. "Thank you."

"I thought you'd be gone long before now."

"Did you?" Cheryl struggled to keep her composure as she opened the truck door.

Merci's hand shot out and grabbed the door. "I think we both know it's time for you to move on. Sam and the girls don't need the help of an outsider."

Cheryl looked the woman in the eye. "I think that's for Sam to decide, not you. I don't like threats—of any kind. That includes the notes you've been sending me."

"I don't know what you're talking about."

"I think you do. Now, if you will excuse me, I have to get back to the ranch." She jerked the door out of Merci's hand,

"You don't belong here. I won't stand by and watch Sam be hurt again." With that, Merci spun on her heels and walked away.

Cheryl sank onto the truck seat, and her shoulders slumped in defeat. Merci was right. It was past time for her to leave. If Dr. Carlton had recognized her resemblance to her mother, then others could, too. She was risking everything she had worked for by staying.

In her head, she knew she should go, but in her heart, she longed to find a way to hold on to the first true taste of happiness she had ever known.

Sam and Walter stood in the barn, watching as Doc Wilson carried the tiny, spotted fawn in from his van. The vet settled the baby on a bed of thick straw and began showing the twins how to bottle-feed him. Sam and Walter stood outside the stall and watched as the girls made over their new pet.

Lindy grinned. "He's so cute."

"We'll call him Bambi," Kayla stated.

"Why does he have spots?"

"Won't Bonkers love him?"

"Can he sleep in our room?"

"Please!" they pleaded together.

Bonkers stalked up to his competition with his tail stiff in the air. He stretched out his neck and sniffed at the fawn with obvious suspicion. The deer sneezed, and Bonkers jumped in fright. Everyone burst out laughing as the cat took off.

Doc slapped Sam's shoulder. "He's your problem now, Sam. If you need me for anything else, just call."

The twins sat cross-legged in the straw and took turns holding the bottle as the fawn nursed eagerly.

"Can Bambi come in the house?" Lindy asked.

"No," Sam stressed. "You aren't to take him outside of this stall. Is that understood?"

"Yes, Daddy." Lindy's lips tightened briefly in a pout.

"What are you going to do with him when he gets too big for the stall?" Cheryl asked from behind them.

"I don't have a clue." Sam smiled at her, feeling foolishly happy. Whenever she was out of his sight, he worried that he'd seen the last of her. Whenever she was near him, he felt as happy and carefree as a kid again.

"If we bottle-raise him, he'll be too tame to turn loose," Walter said.

"Why don't you see if the zoo in Wichita or Kansas City will take him?" she suggested.

"That's a good idea," Walter admitted.

She stepped inside the stall and knelt down. "He is an adorable baby, isn't he?" she said, stroking his sleek head. "Won't he be lonesome out here in the barn?"

The men glanced at each other and rolled their eyes.

"Speaking of babies," Walter said. "What's the latest on Becky?"

"Mom called today," Sam said. "Becky is

still on strict bed rest at home. Mom couldn't give me any idea when she'll be able to come home. It looks like she'll be there until the baby's born. It could be another month."

"Poor Becky," Walter said. "I'll bet she's ready to go nuts staying in bed while Eleanor runs her house."

"I'll bet she is, too," Sam agreed. "Doc, I've got a mare who's overdue. Can you take a look at her for me before you go?"

"Sure."

"It's Flying Lady's first foal, and I'm a little worried." Sam and Walter walked out of the barn with the young vet, and Cheryl stayed behind with the twins.

"What happened to Bambi's mommy?" Kayla asked.

"She ran to safety when the pasture was burned," Cheryl replied, petting the fawn's head.

"Why did she leave her baby behind?"

"I think he was too little to run away, and she knew that we would take care of him."

"Will he miss her?" Lindy asked.

Cheryl stroked his slender neck and watched him guzzle his milk as she pondered her answer. "He will, but not very much if you give him lots of love and attention."

Lindy smiled at Cheryl. "Like you give us?"

"What?" Cheryl's heart stumbled a beat as her glance flew to Lindy's face.

Kayla slipped her arms around Cheryl and laid her head against her side. "You give us lots of love—"

"—like a real mommy does," Lindy added.

Kayla sighed wistfully, "I wish you could be our mommy."

"For real," Lindy said.

A lump rose in Cheryl's throat. A longing she'd been unable to put into words swept over her. She stroked Kayla's soft curls and bent to kiss the top of her head. "Darlings, that's the sweetest thing anyone has ever said to me."

The fawn finished his bottle, and Lindy turned to Cheryl.

"So, why can't you—"

"—stay and be our mother?"

Cheryl stared at their upturned, trusting faces. "It's so complicated."

"Don't you like us?"

Cheryl reached out and drew Lindy close. "Of course I do, it isn't that."

"Is it 'cause you have to be a ballerina?" Kayla asked.

"That's part of the reason."

"Don't ballerinas have kids?" Lindy looked at Cheryl with a puzzled frown.

"Some of them do," Cheryl admitted.

"Then why can't you be our mommy *and* a ballerina?" Kayla insisted. "You could go to work like Daddy does. Grandma would take care of us while you're gone."

"Honey, it isn't that easy." She gazed at their eager faces. Their world was still so simple and so innocent. They would never know a brutal and unkind father because they had Sam. She had no way to make them understand what her life had been like—the shame and humiliation she had known for simply being who she was. The same shame and humiliation that waited for her now if her identity were discovered.

She pulled the girls into a tight embrace. "I can't stay. I wish I could, but I can't. I love both of you very much. Always remember that. Promise me you'll always remember that, no matter what anyone tells you."

"We promise," Kayla said, and Lindy nodded.

Sam watched Cheryl toy with her food at the supper table while the twins talked nonstop about their new pet. They finished the meal quickly and begged to be allowed to go back to the barn. A nod from him sent them running out the door.

"You're quiet tonight, New York. Is your foot bothering you? I noticed you got rid of your cast."

She gave him a weak smile. "It aches a little. This splint is lighter, and I can walk better, but it still leaves something to be desired as far as footwear goes."

"Oh, before I forget, you got a letter today." He rose and searched through the stack of mail by the phone. "Here it is."

She stared at the long, white envelope for a moment, then took it and stuffed it in the pocket of her jeans.

"Do you think you can ride in that splint?" Sam asked.

"Ride?" She shot him a puzzled look.

"I thought we might go for a ride tonight. The moon will be full. It might be fun to try it without the snow. What do you say?"

Her eyes brightened and a smile curved her beautiful mouth. He'd never get tired of seeing her smile, he realized. The phone rang before she could answer him.

"Hold that thought," Sam said and answered the phone.

"Hi, Sam." The sound of Merci's low voice purred in his ear.

"Hi, Merci. What can I do for you?"

"I was wondering if I could catch a ride to the school board meeting with you tonight? My car's in the shop."

"Merci, I don't think I can make it tonight."

"The bond issue is being voted on, Sam. You have to come. We need your support on this."

She was right. He couldn't let his responsibility to the community slide because he wanted to go for a moonlight ride. "Okay, sure, I can give you a lift."

"If it's not too much trouble, that would be wonderful."

Sam glanced at Cheryl. He'd much rather spend the evening with her, but he said, "It's no trouble. I'll see you in thirty minutes."

He hung up the phone and turned to Cheryl. "I'm sorry. I completely forgot about the school board meeting tonight. Maybe we can work in that ride after I get home?"

"Sure."

The brightness left her eyes. She looked down and began to toy with her food again. For a minute, he was tempted to skip his meeting, but his sense of duty got the better of him. The bond issue was important to his children's future.

Cheryl watched Sam leave, then pulled her letter from her pocket and stared at it with dread. The phone rang again, but she let the machine pick up until the sound of a familiar voice made her grab the receiver.

"Angie?" she asked in delight. "Oh, Angie, it's so good to hear your voice."

"I just got your message, Cheryl. What's going on? What are you doing in Council Grove? How bad are you hurt?"

"One question at a time, sis. Where are you?"

"San Francisco. We wanted to spend a few days here before we came back. If Jeff hadn't called home to pick up his messages, I'd still be thinking you were dancing your way across the country. Why didn't you call me? I left you the number of the hotel in Hawaii."

"And ruin your honeymoon? No way."

"Well, thanks for that. But I can't believe you stayed in Council Grove all this time. The sister I know would have crawled on her bloody hands and knees all the way to New York rather than spend one night in Morris County."

"Believe me, I wanted to, but twelve inches of snow nixed that idea. It's a long story, but I ended up staying and playing nanny here on the Hardin ranch."

"Hardin? You don't mean Ol' Hard-as-Nails Hardin from school, do you?"

Cheryl smiled at the once-popular nickname for Sam's stern, no-nonsense mother. "Her son, actually."

"You've got to be kidding! And you as a nanny? I can't believe that."

Cheryl couldn't stop the wistful note in her voice. "It's been wonderful."

"Wonderful?"

"Yeah, wonderful."

"Oh, honey. You've got it bad."

Cheryl didn't pretend to misunderstand. "I've got it bad. For a cowboy with a pair of five-year-old twin girls," she admitted.

"My big sister's in love. It's about time. And what does the cowboy think about it?"

"It doesn't matter."

"Doesn't matter?" Angie exclaimed. "What do you mean, it doesn't matter? Oh, don't tell me he's married!"

"No, of course not."

"So what's the problem? There's nothing wrong with cowboys or ready-made families."

"You know I can't stay here." Cheryl's voice quivered. "I can't face it all again. And besides, I have my career to think about."

"He doesn't know who you are, does he?"

"Does he know he's been sheltering one of the 'thieving Thatchers'? That he's letting a reform-school grad babysit his kids? No, I haven't told him. I've tried, but I can't. I'm such a coward."

"No, you're not. You are the bravest and best sister in the world."

"When will you be home?" Cheryl asked, determined to change the subject.

"Early tomorrow afternoon."

Tomorrow. It would be her last day with Sam and the children. How would she bear it? Sighing, she asked, "Can you put me up for a few weeks?"

"You know I can."

"Don't you think you'd better check with Jeff?"

Angie laughed. "He's still head over heels in love with me. If I say I want you to stay, he'll pretend he's thrilled."

Cheryl had to smile at her sister's confidence. She sobered as she considered how to ask the next question on her mind. There wasn't any easy way to bring up the subject. "Angie, did you know that Jake's out of prison?"

A long silence greeted her question. Finally, Angie said, "Yes, I knew. He was at my wedding."

Cheryl almost dropped the phone. "What? Are you sure? I didn't see him. How did he know about it?"

"Yes, I'm sure," Angie answered calmly.

"Jake knew because I invited him, and you didn't see him because he's as stubborn as you are."

"I don't understand."

"Let's face it, Jake's had the same address for fourteen years. How many letters and visits did he get from you?"

"None," she whispered, ashamed to admit how totally she had cut herself off from her brother.

"He said he wouldn't impose himself on you unless you were willing to see him. He made me promise. I tried to talk to you about him—"

"And I refused to discuss anything about our family. I'm sorry we put you in the middle."

"When I didn't invite him into the dressing room, he simply stayed out of sight in the choir loft. He was the guitarist."

Cheryl sank onto a kitchen chair. Such beautiful, haunting music. "I remember he used to play. I didn't know he was so good."

"There are a lot of things you don't know. Like the fact that he pled guilty and waived his right to trial in exchange for the judge going easy on you."

"What?" Cheryl couldn't believe her ears.

"He made a deal with the district attorney and took the maximum sentence in order for you to get the minimum time."

Cheryl rubbed a hand across her stinging eyes. This was like opening a photo album and seeing the faces of strangers on all the familiar family pictures. Her half brother had sacrificed years of his life to help her. Why?

"I didn't know any of this. Why didn't you tell me?"

"To be honest, I didn't know it either until the last time I went to visit Harriet. Besides, I didn't think you would approve of my staying in contact with Jake. You wanted a clean break with the past. I tried to respect your wishes. Harriet said when you were ready, you'd ask the questions, but until then, you wouldn't be able to hear the answers."

"She was such a wise woman. She was right, I wouldn't have been able to hear anything good about Jake."

"Cheryl, if you're thinking about staying, we need to talk."

"I'm not staying!"

She'd been hiding the truth from Sam for weeks. She couldn't ask him to understand and forgive that. And even if by some chance he did forgive her, she couldn't give up her career to live out here. Sam needed someone to be mother to the twins. She loved the girls, but what kind of mother could she be if she were two thousand miles away? It was a no-win situation.

"We'll talk in person. Not over the phone. Come and get me, Angie."

When Cheryl hung up the phone, she slowly unfolded her letter. It read,

Leave or I'll Make You Sorry.

Chapter Thirteen

Sam held the door open for Merci as they left the high-school gym after the meeting. The full moon had disappeared behind thick clouds, and raindrops dashed any hope he still harbored of a moonlit ride with Cheryl.

"How about some coffee at my place?" Merci asked.

"I don't think so. It's late, I should be getting home."

"I haven't seen much of you lately." Merci laid a hand on his arm. "I've missed you," she said quietly.

Sam found himself at a loss for words.

"Actually," she continued, "I need your professional help with something."

"Are you taking up cattle breeding, Merci?"

She gave a short laugh. "No. I'm going to remodel that dinky house of mine, and I need some advice on which walls I can knock out. I've got the original blueprints at home. Whenever you get some time, maybe you could look at them for me."

The rain began coming down in earnest as Sam gazed at Merci's hopeful face, and his conscience pricked him. Merci had been a good friend to him after his divorce. If her attentions occasionally made him uncomfortable, that was his fault, not hers. He hadn't been ready to resume a relationship with anyone and he knew he had sometimes hurt her feelings.

"Never mind, Sam. It can wait."

"No, I'd be happy to take a look at them for you."

He drove her to her home at the edge of town and followed her through the front door. A high-school-aged girl came out of the living room as they walked in.

"Thanks for babysitting tonight, Susan.

How much do I owe you?" Merci asked, opening her purse.

Susan held out a lock of her waist-length blond hair with a large pink glob in it. "It's free if you know a way to get this gum out of my hair without cutting it. Your son's a brat!"

"Oh, Susan, I'm so sorry." Merci cast Sam an embarrassed look. "He's not really a brat, he's just spirited. Come in to the kitchen. Some peanut butter will take care of this."

"Peanut butter in my hair? How yuck!"

Sam hid a laugh with a cough. "I'll wait in the living room."

Sitting on the sofa, he listened to Susan list the abuses she'd endured. *Brat* sounded like a good description of Jimmy Slader, Jr. The peanut butter worked, but Sam doubted Susan would sit for Jimmy again anytime soon.

He picked up the newspaper while he waited for Susan to leave. With a bark of laughter, he held it up as Merci walked into the room. "I hope you've read it," he said with a smile. It was full of holes, and he wiggled a finger through one.

Merci's eyes widened, and she snatched it away from him. "I can't believe Susan didn't watch him any better than this. She knows not to let him play with scissors."

"I'd say she was lucky to find gum in her hair and not her hair on the floor."

Merci folded the paper into a tight square and sat down on the sofa beside him. "He does it to annoy me—to get attention. He's getting to be a handful. His father never has time for him now that he has a new wife and a baby on the way. What Jimmy needs is a full-time father. You know how it is. Your girls are getting to the age when they need a mother full-time, too."

Sam shifted uncomfortably on the sofa. "Mom does a great job with them."

"Of course she does, but she's not getting any younger. At her age, she should be enjoying herself, not running after the two of them day in and day out."

"She'll let me know when it gets to be too much for her."

"I'm sure she will." Merci smoothed the creases in the paper she held. "I ran into Cheryl Steele at the hospital today. Did she tell you?"

"No, she didn't mention it."

Merci smiled. "She's ready to get out of the boonies and back to New York, isn't she?"

Sam frowned. "Did she say that?"

"You can't blame her. This is a far cry from what she's used to."

"Did she say she wanted to leave?" he insisted.

"Not in those exact words. In fact, she said she was enjoying the diversions ranch life had to offer, but she missed the excitement of the big city and her work."

"I'm sure she does." Sam stared down at his boots. A diversion, was that all he was?

"It was the strangest thing," Merci continued. "Dr. Carter mentioned the Thatcher family, and I swear, she turned as white as a ghost. Why do you suppose that was?"

"I have no idea. Where are those blueprints?" he asked abruptly. He didn't intend to discuss Cheryl with Merci.

It was late when he finally arrived home, but he found himself standing outside Cheryl's room anyway. He raised his fist to knock, but hesitated and lowered his hand.

A diversion. Was he being used to help pass the time and nothing more? He didn't believe that. Their attraction was mutual, he was sure of it. He raised his fist again, but still he hesitated.

An attraction wasn't the same as love. She'd never said anything about love. And neither had he.

Could he risk telling her that he loved her, then watch her walk away as Natalie had done? Could he face that? He stuffed his hands in his pockets.

He'd never considered himself a coward, but this scared him to death. Feeling more confused than ever, he turned away from her door and headed down the stairs.

He was surprised to see Walter lining up a shot at the billiard table when he walked down into the rec room. Sam glanced at his watch. "What are you doing home? I thought you and Fred Barns were on for a game of checkers at the café."

Walter took his shot and sent the cue ball flying down the length of the table. It bounced off the cushion, rolled back and gently kissed the eight ball into the corner pocket.

He picked up his glass of iced tea from the rail and took a drink. "Fred had to leave early.

After that, the company went downhill. Jake Thatcher was there."

"That's funny. Someone else mentioned the Thatchers tonight. Was he making trouble?"

"Not by the time I left. But he rode in on a shiny, new motorcycle. Makes a man wonder where a jailbird gets that kind of money?"

"I hear he's been doing a good job on his grandmother's spread. Cattle prices are up. Maybe he sold some steers."

"Yeah. I wonder who they belonged to? Maybe I should've asked him."

"Don't go looking for trouble, Gramps. A man your age should have more sense."

"Speaking of looking for trouble, isn't that what you're doing?"

"What's that mean?"

Walter walked around the table and began pulling the balls out of the pockets and rolling them to one end. "It means, one day I see you making eyes at a certain blonde, and tonight I see your truck parked outside the house of a certain redhead."

Sam walked to the table and caught the balls Walter rolled his way and placed them in the rack. He picked up a stick. "I wasn't making eyes at anyone. Merci and I are friends. I don't need to defend myself if I want to see her."

Walter lined up the cue ball and made the break. Colored balls careened madly around the table, but none of them dropped into a pocket. "Funny choice of words, *defend*."

Sam took his time as he searched the table for the best shot. He picked a striped ball near the side pocket and sank it with a quick stroke. "Merci wanted me to look at some house plans, that's all." The next ball he tried for stalled at the edge of the pocket. He straightened and watched his grandfather study the table.

Walter missed his next shot. "So which one are you in love with, the blonde or the redhead?"

"Who says I'm in love?"

"That dopey smile you have on your face morning, noon and night. I sure hope it's the redhead."

"Why do you say that?"

Walter straightened and gave Sam a level look. "Because Cheryl doesn't belong here, and you know it."

Sam concentrated on the table for a long

moment. "She could learn to like it. She's great with the girls." He took his turn and missed.

"Sure, she's great with kids, and maybe she even likes it here, but she loves it there." Walter gestured toward the barre and mirror with his chin. "There, she lights up like a hundred-watt bulb."

"She does, doesn't she?" Sam stared at the mirror, picturing Cheryl's smile when she talked about dancing, and the graceful bend and sway of her body as she practiced. If he asked her to stay, he'd be asking her to give up something as essential to her as air. How could he ask her to choose?

Walter sank the rest of the balls on the table, put his stick down, then laid a hand on Sam's shoulder. "I wish she'd leave and get it over with. The longer she hangs around, the harder it's going to be on everyone. I saw you and the kids go through that once, Sam. I'd do anything in my power to keep it from happening again."

"Thanks, Gramps, but I can take care of myself."

"I hope so."

Sam didn't answer him.

Walter turned toward the stairs, then stopped. "Oh, by the way, I was over by the Hazy Creek pasture, and I didn't see hide nor hair of Harvey."

"He was probably hiding, ashamed to be seen with his pedicure."

Walter chuckled. "Maybe. I'll check the water gap tomorrow and make sure the fence isn't down. It wouldn't hurt to call the Double R boys and see if he's slipped over in with their bunch."

"Okay, I'll take care of it in the morning."

"I put Flying Lady in the box stall next to Bambi. I think she'll foal tonight. Want me to check on her before I turn in?"

"If you don't mind."

Walter shook his head. "No trouble."

Sam watched his grandfather disappear up the stairs, then turned his attention to the ballet barre on the wall. Walking up to it, he gripped the smooth wood in his hands and leaned his forehead against the cool mirror.

In his mind's eye he could see how Cheryl looked when she stood poised in the light. It was, he realized, the only time that she let people really see her.

The rest of the time she kept some part of herself hidden. Someone or something must have caused her great pain. He wanted to know what it was. He wanted her to share her burdens as well as her joys with him. She might love dancing, but he knew she cared about him and his girls. He would tell her how he felt—tell her that he loved her—that she made his heart whole again. Tomorrow. He would tell her tomorrow.

With his mind made up, he crossed to his bedroom and softly closed the door.

Sam wasn't in the house when Cheryl rose the next morning. She knocked on his door but there was no reply. The twins lay curled up in their beds still fast asleep. Cheryl closed the door without waking them. After that, she made her way down to the barn.

As she stepped through the barn door, she heard Sam speaking softly from a nearby stall. She walked toward him. He didn't hear her approach. She leaned on the stall door and watched him coax a brown, spindly legged foal to its feet.

His hands and his voice were so gentle, so at odds with his big size and rugged appearance. He glanced up and saw her. A smile lit his face. "'Morning, New York."

"'Morning, cowboy." Her heart contracted and pushed a lump into her throat. She was in love with this man. She opened her mouth to tell him so, but the sound of Walter's voice stopped her.

"What'd she have?" Walter asked as he came to stand beside Cheryl and look over the stall door.

"A nice filly," Sam said, giving her a little help to her feet. "Did you find Harvey?"

"Harvey's missing?" Cheryl asked in surprise.

Walter nodded. "The fences are all good, and I covered that pasture from one end to the other. There's no sign of him and four of our cows are missing, too. I did meet two of the Double R cowboys checking the same fence. It seems they've lost five steers sometime in the past two days."

A deep frown creased Sam's brow. "We'd better notify the sheriff."

"You think he's been stolen?" Cheryl asked. An icy feeling crept into her veins.

Walter slapped his gloves against his thigh. "Looks like it to me. I'll call the sheriff. Then I'm going to pay that thievin' Thatcher a visit to find out what he knows about this."

Cheryl steadied herself against the stall door as the edges of her vision darkened. This couldn't be happening. Not now.

Sam grabbed Walter's elbow. "Don't do anything rash. Let the law handle it."

"It's your best bull, Sam. He's a Grand Champion three times over, and four of your best cows gone with him. Years of breeding work down the drain, not to mention that he's worth thousands of dollars."

"Don't you think I know that? By now they're probably out of the state. If you warn Thatcher that you suspect him, he'll cover his tracks or skip out before the authorities have a chance to investigate."

Walter took a deep breath. "Maybe you're right. What I'd like to know is how he knew where the bull was? Harvey was in that pasture less than twenty-four hours before he was taken."

"Whoever took him must have been watching the place. If I know Sheriff Manning he'll want to check out everyone who's done work for us in the last few months. I've got a list of employees in my office."

Cheryl listened to Sam and Walter in growing horror. Her brother was the first person they suspected. And why not? He'd gone to prison twice for the same crime. It didn't take much of a stretch to think he'd try it a third time. She could find herself tarred with the same brush. She'd be investigated. No one would believe she hadn't been involved, not after she'd kept the truth from them.

She knew how easy it was to look guilty when everyone believed you were. The memory of those long, dark days in the juvenile detention center sent a shiver of fear crawling down her spine.

As much as she loved Sam, she couldn't bear to think of the look on his face when he found out who she was—what she'd been. She couldn't bear it if he thought she was guilty.

Angie would arrive this afternoon unless Cheryl left a message for her at the airport. Sam didn't know she had talked to her sister. It would come as a shock, but maybe it was better this way. Better to make a quick, clean break with no time for a lingering goodbye. No time to watch her dreams fade as she tried to hide how much her heart was breaking.

Sam ran a hand over the stubble of his chin. "Look, I'll go into town and file a report, but I've got a buyer coming in to pick up some yearlings this morning. Can you take care of that for me, Gramps?"

"Are you trying to keep me away from Thatcher?"

"Yes, but more than that, I need your help now."

Walter gave his grudging consent.

"Good." Sam clapped his grandfather on the back. "The paperwork is on my desk." With a nod, Walter left.

Cheryl turned to Sam. "I need to talk."

A smile softened his features. "Good, because there's something I want to tell you."

He reached for her. She gripped his hand for a moment, then released it and clasped her arms across her chest. "My sister called last night."

His smile faded. "Your sister is back?"

"Yes. She's coming to pick me up." She stared at the tips of her shoes. She couldn't bear to watch his face.

After a long pause, he said, "I see. When?"

She heard the bewilderment in his voice, and she knew he didn't understand. "Today. This afternoon."

He turned and took a step away, then spun around to face her. Anguish marred his face. "So, this is goodbye?"

"Yes. You knew I would leave sometime." She wanted so much to reach out and hold him.

He brushed past her and headed for the workbench at the end of the aisle. He opened a cabinet door, then banged it closed and clutched the countertop in front of him. "I thought we might be enough for you, the girls and I."

"I'm sorry, Sam. I can't stay."

He turned to her. "Even if I asked you to? Even if I said—"

"Please, stop. I have to go. We both knew

that at the start. I think we just forgot it for a little while."

He turned away from her. "There isn't much demand for ballet dancers out here, is there?" Bitterness colored his voice with a coldness that chilled her.

Cheryl wished she could find a way to ease the ache in her heart—and in his. Perhaps it would be best to let him believe her career was the reason she was leaving. "I've worked for years to get where I am, Sam. I can't throw it all away."

"I don't know how I could have been so stupid."

"Don't say that. What we had was wonderful. Never doubt it, and please don't belittle it."

Sam turned and stared at her for a long moment. Her pleading was so heartfelt that he knew it wasn't a charade. There was so much pain in her eyes. Why? If her career meant more to her than his affections why would he see so much pain?

"Cheryl, I was afraid of loving someone who didn't love me in return. I thought you were afraid of the same thing. I was wrong, wasn't I? What are you afraid of?"

She turned away, but he caught her hand, preventing her escape. "I love you. I know that you love me and you love my children. I see it in your face every time you look at us. Please, whatever it is, we can work it out. Let me help you."

"Can you change the past, Sam? Can you right the wrongs done by other people? You can't. And I won't let what has happened before touch you or the girls. Please, don't make this any harder for me."

"I wish you could find it in your heart to trust me. Because of you I've learned to love again. I love the way your hair catches the sunlight, the way your eyes sparkle with delight when the girls do something funny. I love the goodness in your soul—the kindness you shower on my family. Why would I want to make it easy for you to leave?"

"If you do love me, you won't try to stop me."

His shoulders slumped in defeat. He dropped her hand. "You win. I can't change the past and whatever happened to you, but

I know you can face it. You can overcome it. Until you are ready to do that, I don't know how to help you."

Cheryl watched him until he stepped out the barn door and closed it behind him, leaving her alone with her heartache. She was a coward. She didn't deserve a man as kind and good as Sam. He and the girls were better off without her. The knowledge brought a fresh stab of grief. She sank to the floor and covered her face as hot tears poured down her cheeks.

Chapter Fourteen

Cheryl managed to regain her composure, and she was in the kitchen when the twins came running upstairs, demanding breakfast. She thought she'd cried out all her tears, but more stung the backs of her eyelids as she watched the girls slide into their chairs at the table. They were dressed in identical blue jeans, yellow Western shirts and blue cowboy hats that hung down their backs by their strings.

"What's for breakfast?" Lindy sniffed. "Pancakes?"

Kayla reached for her juice. "Where's Daddy?"

Cheryl turned the cakes on the griddle. "He had to go into town this morning. I'm making your favorite breakfast—blueberry pancakes."

"Goody."

"Yum."

She slipped the golden-brown pancakes onto plates and took a deep breath before she turned around. She placed a dish in front of each child. "There's something I have to tell you."

"What?" Lindy asked, pouring too much syrup over her stack.

"My sister called me last night. She's home now and I'm going to stay with her for a while."

Kayla stared at Cheryl. "You're going away?"

Cheryl couldn't bear to see the disappointment cloud their faces. She turned away and busied herself at the stove. "Yes, I am."

"But you can't go!" Kayla insisted.

"I have to, sweetheart. I have to get back to my work."

"You can't dance, your foot is still broke," Lindy shouted.

"You said you loved us," Kayla added quietly.

Cheryl spun around and came to kneel beside her. "I do love you."

"Then why do you want to go away?" Kayla whispered. "Did we do something bad?"

"No, of course you didn't."

"Please, don't go. We'll be good, won't we?" Kayla looked at her sister, but Lindy didn't answer.

"I can't stay," Cheryl said as her heart broke into even smaller pieces.

"Are you going back to New York?" Kayla asked quietly.

Cheryl closed her eyes and shook her head. "My sister lives in Wichita. I'll stay with her until the doctor says I can dance again, then I'll leave for New York."

Cheryl struggled to keep the quiver out of her voice. "I thought we could do something really special today, anything you girls wanted. So, what will it be?"

The twins stared silently at each other for a long moment, then Kayla looked at Cheryl and said, "Nothing."

They got up from the table and walked out of the house, the untouched pancakes still on their plates.

Cheryl watched them go. It hurt nearly as much as watching Sam walk away.

She left the kitchen and wandered to the long windows and stared out at the rolling hills. She slid open the balcony door and walked out to lean against the railing. A strong south wind greeted her. The grasses on the hillside across from her nodded and swayed as they danced in the wind.

Walking around the side of the house, she checked on the twins. They were with Walter. A cattle trailer was pulling into the yard and the three of them waited for it beside the barn. Feeling very much alone, Cheryl turned and walked down the hill to the garden.

She hesitated at the stone doorway and gently ran her hand down the moss-covered stones. She leaned her head against them and gazed at the sundial in its circle of flowers. When she left here today she might never hear the sounds of happiness again. The true garden was in her heart, she realized, not on the other side of this stone wall.

Before Sam and his children, her heart had been an empty, barren space. The joy and the pain that came with loving them were both the sunshine and the rain that had made a garden of happiness grow there. Without them, she was afraid only dust would gather in the corners of her heart again. She stepped through the doorway and sat down on the cool stone bench.

She'd wanted to protect Sam and the children, but it seemed all she'd done was hurt them. Was she willing to leave and let those two children spend their whole lives believing they hadn't been good enough to earn her love? Wasn't that the way her father had made her feel?

She loved Sam so much, yet she was willing to let him believe her career meant more to her than his love. That was even worse than failing to tell him the truth about her past. Sam deserved better. She had nothing to do with the missing cattle, but it wasn't fair that all his hard work would be for nothing because of her brother.

Maybe if she went to see Jake, if she could convince him to return the cattle, or at least tell her where he'd sold them, maybe it would help.

She pressed her palms to her temples. What was she thinking? She'd have to go to the ranch. She'd have to face her brother and grandmother and her bitter memories of that place. And why would Jake help her now after she had ignored him for years? Maybe he wouldn't, but she had to try. She owed Sam that much. If only she were as brave as Angie.

Filled with a determination to do what she could to help Sam, Cheryl left the garden without a backward glance.

Walter was saddling a horse beside the barn when she came around the side of the house. There was no sign of Sam. Gathering her courage, she approached his grandfather.

"Walter, I need a favor."

He looked up from his task. "What kind of favor?"

"I need to borrow your truck, and I need you to keep an eye on the girls for me while I—run an errand."

He turned back to the horse and slipped its bridle on. "Can't it wait until Sam gets back?"

"No, it can't."

"What's your hurry?"

"I'm leaving today."

That snapped his head around. "Does Sam know?"

"Yes."

He nodded toward the twins climbing on the corral fence. "Do they?"

"Yes, I told them. My sister is coming for me this afternoon."

Walter stared at her for a long moment. "Take the truck. The keys are in it. I think I'm going to miss you."

"I might just miss you, too, Walter." She smiled at him sadly. Turning away, she crossed the yard, climbed in the truck and drove out of the yard.

Lindy, sitting on the top rail of the fence, banged boot heels against the boards in frustration. "She can't leave. I don't want her to. I thought she wanted to be our mother."

"She does."

"She does not!"

"She does, too!"

"What are you arguing about?" Walter asked as he rode up next to them.

"Nothing," they answered together.

"Well, pipe down. You'll scare the cattle," he said.

"Where's Cheryl going? I didn't say goodbye." Kayla started to climb down from the fence as Cheryl drove past.

"She's got an errand to run. She's not leaving until her sister gets here. You'll have plenty of time to say goodbye." He entered the corral and began cutting two young bulls away from the herd and driving them toward the loading chute.

"We got to find a way to stop her," Lindy said more quietly. She pushed her hat off and let it dangle down her back by the ties.

"Daddy will stop her."

"What if she leaves before he comes home? Then what will happen?"

"I don't know," Kayla admitted.

They watched silently as Walter loaded the first two cattle into the trailer, then he rode back into the herd and began to cut two young heifers away and drive them up the chute. The truck driver lowered the gate with a loud clatter when the last calf entered the trailer. He came and stood beside the girls.

"Fer a minute there, I thought I was a seein' double," he drawled, tipping his hat back. "Don't folks have trouble tellin' you apart?"

The twins nodded. "Yup," they answered together.

"Where are you—"

"—taking Daddy's cattle?"

He spat a stream of tobacco juice on the ground. "Yer daddy sold 'em, so they ain't his cattle no more. The heifers I'm takin' to a ranch over by Abilene, and them bulls are going to a farm down by Wichita."

"Wichita?" Lindy looked at her sister and smiled. Kayla stared at her a moment, then nodded slowly.

"Yup, all the way to Wichita," the man replied.

Walter rode up, dismounted and looped his

reins over the fence. "Come to the house, Mr. Reed, and we'll settle the bill."

The two men crossed the yard together. They stepped apart as Bonkers darted between them and scampered toward the twins still sitting on the fence.

Cheryl turned the pickup off the highway at the familiar corner and drove slowly down the rutted lane. Weeds sprouted in a wide path between the tire tracks. The house, when it came into view, was as neglected-looking as the lane.

The once-white building was gray with age and peeling paint. The porch railing was missing a spindle or two giving the house the appearance of an old hag with missing teeth. It seemed smaller than she remembered. The yard was overgrown and wore an air of neglect.

Only the barn and corrals showed signs of repairs. A battered green-and-white pickup held a stack of new lumber and paint cans that showed someone's intent to continue the work.

Cheryl stepped out of the truck and waited.

There was no sign of life. She approached the house with trepidation and climbed the steps. The front door stood open behind the screen door. She didn't have any idea what she'd say to Doris or to Jake, but she raised her hand and knocked as loudly as her wavering courage would allow. No one came. Calling out a hello, she opened the door and stepped inside her childhood home.

Little had changed, she saw as she stood in the entryway. The wallpaper was the same pattern of yellow roses, now faded to a drab gray. A glance into the living room showed her the same brown sofa, sagging more in the middle, and an overstuffed chair. The smell was different, she thought. It smelled old and devoid of life. It all seemed so familiar, and yet so foreign.

"Hello?" she called out again. Only silence answered her. Her sense of unease grew. She turned and hurried toward the front door and the fresh air and sunshine. Her hand was on the screen door when a dark figure loomed in front of her, blocking out the light.

"What are you doing here?"

For an instant, she didn't recognize his

voice. Older and deeper, it carried a hard edge that sent a chill down her spine. So this was the man her brother had become. Fear flickered in the pit of her stomach. What had made her think that she could confront him? No one knew where she'd gone.

The thought of Sam and what he stood to lose stiffened her spine. Jake wasn't going to ruin all Sam had worked to achieve. Not if she could help it.

Raising her chin, she said, "I wouldn't have come at all if you hadn't stolen Harvey. Where is he? I want him back." She shoved open the screen door.

"Who?" He stepped backward as she barged out of the house.

She held her arms outstretched as she advanced on him. "Big white bull." She wiggled her fingers over her head. "Lots of curls. Pink hooves that match these." She thrust her nails in front of his face.

"I don't know what you're talking about." He took another step back and teetered on the edge of the steps.

Shoving against his chest with both hands, she sent him sprawling in the dirt. His black hat went flying. She straddled his body before he could get up. Balling her fists, she said, "You tell me where he is or I'll—I'll…"

A slow grin spread over his face, softening his features into the charming older brother she'd once known. "Or you'll do what? Spit in my eye? If I remember right, Twiggy, that's what you used to threaten me with."

Her bravado evaporated at his use of the nickname she'd hated. She dropped her fists.

"After all this time you can't even say hello?" he asked.

Slowly, she extended one hand toward him. "Hello, Goat Breath. How have you been?"

"Not too bad." After a moment, he took her hand, and she pulled him to his feet. "Nobody's called me Goat Breath in a long, long time. Sounds kind of nice."

Cheryl sank onto the porch steps behind her, and after a brief hesitation, he picked up his hat and sat down beside her.

"You didn't take them, did you?" she said.

"Take what?"

"Sam Hardin's cattle."

"No." He dusted off his hat.

"They think you did. The sheriff will be out here soon."

He settled his hat on his head. "It won't be the first time. But there's nothing for him to find."

She stared at Jake, seeing how the years had added lines to his face. He hadn't had an easy time of it. "I'm sorry I suspected you."

He shrugged. "Can't blame you. My track record ain't exactly flawless." He returned her steady regard. "You sure look like your mother."

"So I've been told."

"She was always good to me. I loved her for that. What are you doing out here, Cheryl?"

"I had a car accident on my way to Manhattan after Angie's wedding, and I broke my foot. The rest is a long story, but I've been staying at the Hardin ranch. Angie told me you were at her wedding. Your music was beautiful."

"Yeah, well, I had plenty of time to practice."

"Angie also told me yesterday about what you did for me. If it means anything after all this time—thank you."

He scuffed the ground with the heel of his boot. "Yeah, it means something."

"I wish… I'm sorry I didn't…you know… keep in touch."

"After the mess I got you into, I didn't expect you would."

"No, it wasn't right that I cut you off. I'm glad Angie had more sense. Our little sister is a lot deeper than I thought."

He nodded. "She's a good kid. I hope she's happy with Jeff."

"I think she will be. What about you? Is there anyone?"

His bark of laughter was bitter. "In this cattle country? No rancher's daughter is going to take a chance on me. Besides, I've been too busy trying to make a go of this place."

"Looks like you're making progress."

"Like you didn't know."

She frowned. "How would I know?"

He stood and shoved his hands in his pockets. "It may take a while, but I can get this place back on its feet. You'll see."

What had she said to upset him? She stood and placed a hand on his shoulder. "I'm sure you will." She smiled and gave him a gentle shake. "Although, it's just like a cowboy to fix up the barn before he fixes up the house."

"Doris won't let me touch the place. I've got a room down in the barn. I stay there and keep an eye on her. She's gotten more peculiar in her old age. She was doing a little better until she saw you."

Astounded, Cheryl said, "She saw me? When?"

"You were in Council Grove at the doctor's office after that snowstorm. It's a small town. It didn't take her long to find out Hardin had a strange woman staying on his ranch. Doris kind of went off the deep end then."

He turned to her and gripped Cheryl's shoulders. "She doesn't have anywhere else to go. She doesn't have any money. She's an old woman. I know she treated you badly when you were a kid—"

"Badly?" Cheryl jerked out of his hold and took a step away. "I can't tell you how many times she took a belt to my back. Believe me, almost a year in the girls' correctional facility was a walk in the park compared to life here."

"She beat you?"

Of course he hadn't known. She'd never told anyone, and it wasn't fair to blame him now. She crossed her arms and stared at the ground. "After Mom died and Doris came to live with us, you got your own place. And Dad was so drunk most of the time, he didn't care. She and I didn't get along from the get-go. I was mouthy and surly and mad at the world. She couldn't stand the way I acted out."

"That didn't give her the right to hit you."

"After I came back from juvie, it got a lot worse. Doris blamed me because that stupid diary I kept was the reason Dad and you were caught and went to prison the second time."

Jake shook his head. "The crimes we committed sent us to prison, honey."

"The sheriff would never have known where we were if I hadn't written about keeping the cattle out at the old Stoker place. If I hadn't gloated about what we got away with."

"I don't blame you. I never did. I never should have let Dad drag you into the business in the first place."

"I wanted to help. I wanted him to notice

me, to love me. Kids will do stupid things to get noticed, won't they? In the end maybe I was more like him than I thought."

Jake drew her into a fierce hug. "No, kid. You've got too much of your mother in you to end up like him, or like me."

Tears stung her eyes as she returned his hug. "Thanks, but I don't think you turned out so badly," she muttered against his shirtfront.

He held her at arms' length. "No, but it took me a long time to decide which way I was going to go. I met a good man in prison. He was a counselor. He told me about finding forgiveness. I've been trying to live the way he taught me. It hasn't been easy. If Sam Hardin wants to find his missing cattle, tell him to look for a cowhand that was fired from the Double R about a week ago."

"How do you know this?"

He gave her a wry smile. "The sheriff isn't the only one who thinks I practice my old trade. Now and then I get offers."

She managed a smile in return. "Thank you. Where is Doris? It's past time she and I set a few things straight."

"You just missed her. She left a little while

ago with a woman named Slader. They didn't say when they'd be back."

The earth shifted beneath Cheryl as a loud buzzing filled her ears. "Do you mean Merci Slader?"

"A tall redhead, doesn't smile much. Hey, you're as pale as a sheet. What's wrong?" He steadied her with both hands.

"Oh, no. I should have told him." She pulled away from Jake and hurried to her pickup.

"Cheryl, wait! What's wrong?" He followed her and laid a hand on the open window as she started the engine.

"I never told Sam who I really am. Don't you see? They've gone to tell him about me. If he gets back before I do, he'll know I kept the truth from him all this time. I'm sorry, Jake, I have to go." She put the truck in gear and sped away.

Sam turned into his lane, and the image of Cheryl as he had last seen her flashed into his mind for the hundredth time. Had he imagined the regret and longing that had filled her eyes? He knew that he loved her. He couldn't, wouldn't, believe she didn't love him in return. Had she left already? He didn't know which he dreaded more, finding her gone or watching her leave.

When he pulled up in front of the house, he saw Merci Slader's dark blue Sable parked beside it. What did she want?

Walter came out of the house as Sam stepped out of the truck. "That took you long enough. How'd it go?"

"Our report's been filed. The sheriff wants to talk to the foreman at the Double R before he questions anyone else."

"He'd better make it fast. The longer he waits, the less chance we have of getting our cattle back."

"I know." Sam stared at the front door of the house. He wanted to see Cheryl coming out to greet him, to tell him she'd made a mistake and she intended to stay. Something in his face must have given him away.

"She's not here," Walter said quietly, his eyes full of sympathy. "She borrowed my truck. Said she had an errand that couldn't wait. Her sister called and left a message to say she was on her way."

"I see. Where are the girls?" he managed to ask.

Walter looked around the yard. "I'm not sure. They were here a little while ago. I thought they had gone to the house, but they're not inside."

"Has she told them she's leaving today?"

"Yes."

"Did they seem upset?"

"Not when I saw them."

"Maybe they're down in the garden." Sam shoved his hands into the pockets of his jeans. "Well, Gramps. This is where you get to say, 'I told you so.'"

Walter laid a hand on Sam's shoulder. "I think I'd rather say I'm sorry it turned out this way."

"Thanks."

Walter nodded. "Merci Slader is waiting to talk to you."

"I saw her car. Did she say what she wanted?"

"No, she wouldn't talk to me. She has Doris Thatcher with her. Said you'd want to hear what the woman had to say."

Chapter Fifteen

Cheryl parked the truck beside the barn. Sam stood on the front porch watching her. She crossed the distance between them with lagging steps, feeling her courage ebb away. She knew by the look on his face that she was too late. She could only hope that he would understand why she had deceived him.

She stopped at the foot of the steps. The silence stretched between them. She rubbed her palms on the side of her jeans. "Sam, I can explain."

Merci stepped out of the doorway behind Sam. "I hope you enjoyed your little joke, Ms.

Steele. Or should I say, Ms. Thatcher. You really had us fooled. There's hardly a trace of the poor little country girl left." Cheryl's grandmother came out of the house and stood beside Merci.

"So it's true? You're a Thatcher?" Sam asked.

Cheryl's heart sank at the sight of his expression. The pain and disbelief in his eyes told her more than words how much her deception had hurt him. "Yes, it's true."

Merci gave her a frosty smile. "You should have told us who you were. You're quite famous around here. It's not every day a girl of twelve steals a semitrailer-load of cattle, and then rides down the officer trying to arrest her. Walter said you've had some cattle stolen recently, Sam. Perhaps Ms. Thatcher can explain how that happened?"

"I knew she was no good. She's here to make trouble and nothing else," Doris Thatcher announced. Dressed in a faded, black, shapeless garment, her gray hair drawn back in a tight bun, she looked every one of her seventy-odd years. "I tried to change the children from their evil ways, but my words fell on deaf ears."

Cheryl studied Sam's face. Did he truly think she had helped steal his cattle? She straightened as she faced him. She'd spent a lifetime being ashamed of who and what she was—hiding from her own past. But she was more than Hank Thatcher's daughter—a lot more. She was also Mira Thatcher's daughter. Something she would be proud of until her dying day. If Sam Hardin didn't see that after all they'd meant to each other, she wasn't going to beg him to understand.

"Excuse me, I have to finish packing." She marched up the steps, and the group at the top parted as she walked between them with her head held high.

She was halfway across the living room when Sam caught her arm and turned her to face him. "Why didn't you tell me the truth?"

Pride kept her back straight when what she wanted to do was fall into his arms. "I started to a dozen times, Sam, but I knew how people would react." She gestured toward the door. "Just like that. It doesn't matter what I've done or where I've been for the last fifteen years. All that matters is that Hank Thatcher was my father and that must make me a thief."

"Cheryl, I don't believe you had anything to do with my missing cattle."

"Thank you. But others won't be so kind. My mother was a good, decent woman who never hurt anyone. All she did was try to survive a bad marriage and shelter her children. For that, she never got anything from her so-called friends and neighbors except condemnation. I didn't expect anything different."

"I'm not condemning you, Cheryl, but I thought you trusted me."

Cheryl heard the pain in Sam's voice. "I do trust you, but try to understand. I wanted you to see *me.* I didn't want who you saw to be colored by who I was. I never meant to hurt you."

Her grandmother advanced toward them, her thin frame shaking with emotion as she yelled, "You should never have come back. I told your sister, and I'm telling you—go away. You can't steal what rightly belonged to my son. The place is mine."

Cheryl studied her grandmother's worn

face. She and Angie had escaped into new lives, but Doris Thatcher had stayed and faced the whispers and the snubs of this community all these years. She'd been in a prison as surely as Jake had been, only the bars were ones you couldn't see. No wonder she seemed crazed by it all.

"I don't know what you're talking about, Grandma."

"That's a lie. You've come to drive me out of my home."

Sadly, Cheryl shook her head. "No, I haven't. I couldn't, even if I wanted to."

"Actually, you could," a crisp new voice declared.

Every head turned in surprise as Eleanor Hardin walked into the room. Setting her suitcase on the floor, she crossed the room to stand in front of Cheryl.

"So you're Sam's ballerina. Oh, you've grown to look so much like your mother. I'm very glad to see you again, my dear."

"Hello, Mrs. Hardin," Cheryl whispered.

Eleanor turned away from Cheryl and faced the others in the room. "Everyone sit down," she commanded in her usual brusque manner. "I want to hear the whole story from the start."

Eleanor crossed to Sam. "Close your mouth, Samuel. You look like an astonished fish." She reached up, pulled his head down, and gave him a quick kiss on the cheek. "Did you miss me?" she asked softly.

"I wasn't expecting you for another month."

"Becky's mother-in-law came to help out. The house wasn't big enough for the both of us."

"How is Becky?"

She flashed him a bright smile. "I think she was a little glad to see me go. Doris, don't you dare leave," Eleanor called as Cheryl's grandmother gave a huff and turned on her heels.

"She can't take my home!"

"She can if she wants it. That was the deal."

Confused, Cheryl glanced from one woman to the other. "I don't understand. What deal?"

"Tell her," Eleanor commanded.

"It was blackmail, that's what it was," the old woman spat.

"Maybe, but Harriet was smart enough to make it legal."

Cheryl stared at Sam's mother in amazement. "You knew Harriet?"

Eleanor nodded. "Your mother, Harriet and I were close friends as girls together. Harriet's parents died when she was a baby. She came to live with your mother's family on the same ranch you grew up on. Your mother's father was a wise man. He wanted to make certain that both girls were taken care of after he was gone. He had the ranch placed in a trust for them.

"Harriet strongly disapproved of your father, but Mira loved him, and she married him over everyone's objections. She and Harriet had a falling-out over it, and Harriet moved to Philadelphia. She told me later that she regretted cutting herself off from Mira."

Doris interrupted her. "The ranch should have gone to my son. He was her lawful husband. It wasn't right that they kept it from him."

"But it was smart," Eleanor shot back. "Hank would have lost the place in no time."

Cheryl struggled to understand. "You mean the ranch belonged to Harriet after my mother died?"

Eleanor nodded.

"And now?"

"It's part of a trust that Harriet set up for you and Angela. Harriet was willing to let your father live on the ranch and raise you there. It wasn't until after your father died, and I contacted Harriet with my suspicions about your grandmother's treatment of you, that Harriet and I hatched this plan."

"*You* contacted Harriet?"

"Yes. Your grandmother was your legal guardian, but Harriet owned the property. In exchange for transferring legal guardianship to Harriet, Doris was allowed to remain on the ranch for the rest of her life, or until either you or Angela expressed a desire to return and live there."

"The income I get from Harriet's trust fund comes from the ranch?"

"That and other investments Harriet made. I thought you knew. Your sister knows about it."

Cheryl nodded. "She would. She and Harriet's lawyer were co-executors of Harriet's estate. I was so wrapped up in my career that

I never even asked where the money came from."

No wonder her grandmother hadn't wanted her to come back. She must have been afraid of being driven out of her home.

"The place is yours if you want it," Eleanor said quietly.

"No," Doris wailed. "She can't have it. Where will I go?" She sank onto the sofa and began to rock back and forth.

Cheryl watched Sam turn his back to the room and stare out the window. She had thrown away her chance at happiness here because she'd been ashamed. She had lacked the courage to share her past with Sam. He had no reason to trust her now.

"I don't want the ranch or any part of it," she said.

Sam stared out the window feeling heartsick. When Merci had confronted him with Cheryl's deception, all he could think about was how his wife had deceived him. How he'd been played for a fool again. Had Cheryl cared for him even a little? He didn't know what to think.

"Let Doris and Jake stay," Cheryl told his mother. "I have my career, and that's more than enough."

Sam shoved his hands in his pockets and closed his eyes. He had his answer from her own lips. She didn't want any part of them. Could he blame her?

"Are you sure? It was your home," Eleanor said gently.

When Cheryl didn't answer, Sam turned and met her gaze across the room. "I'm sure," she said. "There's nothing for me here."

Walter walked into the room then, and stopped short at the sight of Eleanor. "What are you doing here?"

"I came home early."

"Are the twins with you? I can't find them anywhere."

Sam frowned in concern. "What do you mean you can't find them? When was the last time you saw them?"

"They watched me load cattle this morning," Walter answered.

"The letters," Cheryl exclaimed.

Sam turned to her. "What letters?"

Cheryl strode up to her grandmother.

"You sent them, didn't you? Where are the children? If you've hurt them—"

Doris shrank before Cheryl's anger. "I don't know what you're talking about."

"What letters?" Sam demanded again.

"Someone sent me threatening notes, telling me to leave or I'd be sorry."

"Do you still have them?"

Cheryl nodded. She hurried out of the room, returned with the papers and handed them to Sam.

He glanced at each sheet, then fixed his eyes on Merci. "What do you know about these?"

"Me?" she asked in obvious surprise.

"You were adamant about getting Cheryl to leave."

Merci glared at him. "I know nothing about her notes. I came here today because I thought you should know the truth about that woman. I'd never threaten your children."

Sam turned his gaze on the elderly woman on the sofa. "That leaves you, Mrs. Thatcher."

"I don't know anything."

He advanced until he towered over her and

held the letters in front of her face. "Did you send these?"

She cringed away from him. "I wanted her to leave, that's all. She can't drive me away from my home."

"Where are my children?" he bit out.

Eleanor sat down beside the trembling woman. "Sam, calm down. Doris, tell us everything."

Doris kept her eyes down. "I sent the notes, but that's all. I haven't seen your girls."

Cheryl studied her grandmother's face for a long moment, then sat down beside her. "You were very cruel to me. No child deserved to be treated the way you treated Angie and I."

Doris glanced at her, but quickly looked away. "Your dad was an only child. My husband used to say I spoiled the boy, but I didn't believe it. Then, look how he turned out. I was ashamed to call him my son, but I still loved him.

"I didn't want you to turn out like he did. I thought I could beat some sense into you, but you were so stubborn. Then that stupid diary of yours sent him to prison. He died there! My son died without me by his side.

You took away my son and now you want to take away my home."

Cheryl sat back and stared at her grandmother. She thought of all the fear and shame this woman had caused and she wanted to hate her, but all she felt was pity. She took a deep breath, hoping the right words would come. "Someday, I hope we can find a way to get past the anger and bitterness of those years. I was a lonely, scared kid with no one to confide in, so I wrote down the things I couldn't tell you or anyone. I was angry at the world and I wanted to hurt someone as much as I was hurting. I wanted my dad to pay attention to me so I did the one thing he was sure to notice. I helped him steal cattle from our neighbors.

"I don't know how Angie found my diary or why she took it to school with her. I don't even know how Mrs. Hardin wound up with it."

Eleanor gave her a sad smile. "One of the boys at school, a bully, his name doesn't matter, took her book bag and dumped it out on the playground. I saw what happened and came to help her pick up her papers. The book had fallen open to the last entry you had made. I couldn't help seeing what you wrote. I *had* to tell the sheriff."

"I know. I understand. Grandmother, you have my word that you can stay at the ranch for as long as you like, only please tell us where the twins are."

"I don't know. I don't know." She burst into tears.

Eleanor sat beside the weeping woman. "I believe you, Doris. It will be okay. Merci will take you home, now."

"I'd rather stay and help find the girls," Merci announced.

Eleanor raised one eyebrow. "You brought her here, you should take her home. I think you've helped enough for one day." There was no mistaking the order in her quiet tone.

Merci helped the still-weeping woman to her feet and they left together.

"Sam, where could the girls be?" Cheryl asked, sick with worry.

He raked a hand through his hair. "A hundred places. Let's spread out and check everywhere again. Check every cupboard and closet."

Nodding, Eleanor and Cheryl began searching the house while the men searched outside.

"Anything?" Eleanor asked when they met up with Walter and Sam by the barn door.

"Nothing," Sam said. "How could two little girls disappear without a trace? Has anyone else been here?"

"Only the cattle buyer," Walter answered.

"How well do you know him?" Cheryl asked, her voice tight.

Sam looked at her in disbelief. "What are you saying?"

"I'm asking, how well do you know the man?" she snapped.

"Elmer Reed picked up the cattle," Walter answered.

"Where was the trailer headed, and when did it leave?" Sam asked, trying to rein in his growing fear.

"He was going to drop the heifers off in Abilene and then deliver the bulls to a ranch down by Wichita. He left an hour ago."

"Wichita? Did the girls know where the trailer was going?" Cheryl demanded.

Walter nodded. "Yes, I heard Reed tell them where he was taking the cattle."

"I told the twins that I would be staying with my sister in Wichita. Could they have gotten into the trailer without the driver knowing it?"

Walter shook his head. "They wouldn't be able to get in back with the cattle. There's no way they could lift the end gate. The trailer did have a side compartment, but they're too little to reach the door handle."

Cheryl's gaze flew to the bucket sitting a few feet away, and she pointed. "What if they stood on that?"

Sam followed her across the yard. Small muddy boot prints and paw prints decorated the top of an overturned white plastic five-gallon bucket.

"This is where the trailer was parked, wasn't it?" Cheryl looked to Walter and back to Sam.

"Okay." Sam bowed his head a moment. He had to think straight, he couldn't let his fear get in the way. "Walter, get the information on where those cattle are being delivered. Call the people and let them know what's going on. The trailer should be almost to Abilene by now. Then notify the Highway Patrol and have them start looking for it. Mom, check with the neighbors to see if anyone has seen the girls. This may turn out to be a wild goose chase. If it is, we'll need to organize a search party and have them spread out from the ranch on foot." He started toward his truck.

"Where are you going, Sam?" his mother called after him.

"I think Cheryl is right. I think they hitched a ride to Wichita on that trailer. I'm going to try and catch up with them. Walter, raise me on the radio if you hear anything."

"Right."

Cheryl hurried after Sam. He had started the pickup by the time she yanked open the door. He glared at her as she climbed in. "What do you think you're doing?"

She slammed the door closed. "I'm coming with you."

"No, you're not."

"You don't have time to drag me out of here, so drive."

"Your sister will be here soon."

"She'll wait."

He hesitated an instant, then he shoved the truck into gear and tore out of the yard.

He flew down the highway well over the legal speed limit. Several times, he glanced at Cheryl. She sat silent and tight-lipped beside him, a worried frown etched on her face. Twenty minutes later, he slowed for the wide spot in the road that was the town of Delavan. Cheryl continued to stare straight ahead, but he saw her lip quiver before she bit down on it.

"Are you okay?" he asked.

"Yes."

His grip tightened on the wheel. "Why didn't you tell me the truth?"

She fixed her gaze on him. "At first, because I thought I would be gone in a day or two, and it wouldn't matter."

"And later?"

She looked away. "Later, I was afraid that it would matter."

"I wish you had trusted me."

She sighed. "What was I supposed to say? 'Oh, by the way, did I mention my family used to steal cattle, and I spent time in jail for helping?' That's a little hard to work into after-dinner conversation." She stared down at her hands. "I thought if you found out, you wouldn't want me near the girls."

"I thought we had more going for us than after-dinner conversation." He couldn't help the bitterness that crept into his voice.

"I'm sorry. You're right. The truth is—I was trying to protect myself. Running away, hiding from my past had become an ingrained habit. You can't imagine what it was like, being mocked and worse because my name was Thatcher. I wanted to bury who I was and never dig her up. You helped me see that I had to face my past. You showed me how to live. I wanted to be a woman like that. That's why I went to see Jake today. I was coming back to tell you everything. I never wanted to hurt you, or the children. If you can't believe anything else, I hope you'll believe that."

"I do."

She raked a hand through her hair. "I shouldn't have let them out of my sight. I knew how upset they were."

"This isn't your fault." He shook his head. "If they hadn't hitched a ride on this trailer, they would've hatched some other harebrained plan."

A small grin lifted some of the worry from her face. "They *are* imaginative."

He tried for a lighter tone. "Do me a favor, will you? When you're back in New York, keep an eye out for them. There's no telling how soon they'll think of a way to visit you."

"Maybe their father could bring them," she suggested softly.

He glanced at her. "Yes, maybe he could."

Hope began to unfurl in Cheryl's heart. Sam had been hurt by the way she had deceived him, but perhaps he could forgive her, in time.

She stared straight ahead. The highway ran west in a long silver ribbon between vast stretches of prairie. In most places, the hills were little more than acres of charred ground where the spring fires had swept across them. Boulders and stones protruded from the burnt ashes like white bones, but here and there, new green life was beginning to show as the resilient grass sprouted again.

The bright sunlight dimmed, and she realized towering thunderheads had blocked out the afternoon sun. The radio crackled as Walter's voice came on. "Sam, do you read me? Over."

Sam picked up the mike and answered him. "Go ahead, Walter."

"The trailer arrived in Abilene twenty minutes ago. The twins had been in it, but they must have gotten out somewhere along the route. All they found was one of their hats in the feed compartment."

"Did the driver say where he stopped?"

"We figure he made about eight stops, mostly at intersections. Three of those would be in towns along the route, three would be rural intersections. He says he stopped once for a train on Highway Fifteen and once at a narrow bridge to let a combine go through. He thinks that was on this side of Herington, but he can't be sure."

"Eight stops in sixty miles. That doesn't narrow the search much."

"The Highway Patrol and the county sheriff are questioning him now. They'll start working their way back from Abilene to here."

"Okay. We're just west of Delavan, Walter. Keep us posted." Sam turned on the wipers as big drops splattered the windshield.

"We'll find them, Sam. I know we will."

Cheryl didn't know if she was trying to reassure Sam or herself.

Like a hamster on an exercise wheel, her mind ran over and over all the dire possibilities. They could have been picked up by anyone—a kindly farmer or a dangerous stranger. They could be scared and hiding so that even the right people couldn't find them. She tried to ignore the possibility that they might have tried to jump out of the moving trailer and be lying injured in a ditch somewhere along this road. Her eyes searched through the rain-streaked glass for any sign of them as Sam drove westward.

The storm brought an early gloom to the late afternoon. Sam turned on the headlights. The road curved then dipped down to cross a narrow creek. Their headlights swung past an old abandoned church falling into ruins in a grove of trees at the road's edge. A yellow cat sat licking its paw on the sagging railing of a little portico. The passing headlights reflected briefly in its eyes.

Cheryl twisted around in her seat. "Sam, did you see that?"

Chapter Sixteen

Sam braked the truck sharply. "What did you see?"

"Bonkers is back there on the church steps."

"Are you sure?"

"Yes—no! I don't know. It was a big, yellow cat. Please, we have to go check."

He turned the truck on the narrow highway and drove back, but the headlights revealed only an empty porch.

"I know it was Bonkers." Cheryl opened the door, and shouted for the twins.

"Cheryl, get in. You're getting soaked. We

aren't near any of the places the driver said he stopped. There must be a hundred yellow cats between here and Abilene."

"I tell you, Sam, it was Bonkers." Determined to prove she wasn't mistaken, Cheryl crossed the overgrown churchyard and started up the dilapidated steps.

She tried the front door. It opened a few inches, but stuck fast on the warped wooden floor. From inside, she heard a faint meow. "Lindy? Kayla? Are you in there?"

"Cheryl, is—"

"—that you?"

Relief poured through her at the sound of their voices. "Sam, they're in here."

He was beside her in an instant. "Are you girls all right?" he called.

"Yes, Daddy."

"Can you come and get us?"

"They're all right." Relief made Cheryl light-headed.

Sam grabbed the wedged door and pulled, but stopped when a loud groaning sound issued from the building overhead. "I can't get in, girls. Can you get out?"

"No, the floor fell down."

"All by itself."

"We didn't do it."

Sam stepped back and began to look for another way in. Moving around to the side of the building, he saw that the center section of the roof had fallen in and bare rafters jutted out like broken ribs. The steeple and the ends of the building leaned precariously inward. He listened to the old boards creaking and groaning in the rising wind.

A streak of lightning flashed and thunder rolled in an ominous cadence across the prairie as the grove of trees around them bent low in a gust of wind. He glanced in fear at the slanting steeple of the old church. He had to get the girls out.

On the north side of the building, he found a large section of the wall had fallen in, and he made his way toward the gaping hole. The ground around the church lay littered with piles of old junk.

He stopped at the hole and peered in through the fallen wall. It took a moment for his eyes to adjust to the gloom. Years ago, someone had pulled up the floorboards and left only the floor joists in place. They stretched like an empty tic-tac-toe game above a deep cellar. A small section of the roof had caved in and caught on them. The twins sat huddled on a few fallen boards almost directly across the building from him.

Between him and the girls stood thirty feet of empty space. Below them lay a hazard-filled pit.

People had been using the cellar of the abandoned church as a junk heap for decades. Scrap lumber, hundreds of broken bottles, rusted tin cans, rolls of barbed wire, broken bits of farm machinery and assorted debris covered the deep cellar floor.

"Daddy, come get us," Lindy called as she sat with her arms around Kayla. Bonkers lay beside them.

"Okay, honey, I will. Just stay still." Sam searched for a way to reach them. "How did you get out there?"

"We followed Bonkers in, but the floor fell down, and we couldn't get back. I told Kayla we could walk out like Bonkers did on those boards, but she's scared. She thinks she'll fall."

He blanched at the thought of the girls

trying to walk across the old beams above the wreckage-filled pit. The gusty wind would make the trip dangerous even for the cat. There had to be a better way.

"Stay there, girls, don't move," he called. "I'll come and get you."

But how? Desperately, he studied the wreck of a building looking for a way to reach his children. The rain fell in earnest now. Dropping to one knee beside him, Cheryl began to undo the splint on her ankle.

"What are you doing?" he asked.

"I'm going to walk over there and carry them out, but I can't do it with this splint on," she answered, working the straps loose.

Sam dropped beside her and grasped her wrist, stopping her. "Are you crazy? Did you look down there? Even if that old wood is strong enough to hold you, you can't do it on a broken foot. If you fall into that junk heap, you'd be lucky to walk again, let alone dance." The driving rain soaked both of them as they stared at each other.

"Have you got a better idea?" she asked. "You're the architect. Will that roof hold if the wind gets worse?"

He looked at the old bell tower leaning inward over the sagging roof and shook his head. "I can't see what's keeping it up now. It looks like it would come down if a pigeon landed on it."

"I can do this, Sam."

He studied her face for a long moment. He didn't see fear or hesitation, only determination in the bright blue eyes that stared back at him. She was willing to do this for his children. She was willing to risk her career, maybe even her life. Another strong gust of wind drove the rain into his face, and he wiped it away with his hand. Lightning flashed close by, followed by the sharp crack of thunder. The old building gave a creaking moan as it shifted.

"How can I let you do this?" he muttered.

"Hey, cowboy, the question is, how are you going to stop me?"

He gazed at her and knew she was telling the truth. She loved his daughters enough to risk everything for them.

Thunder rumbled again in the leaden sky, and Sam rose to his feet. "I've got a rope.

Maybe I can rig a safety line for you." He turned and ran for the truck.

"Hurry, Sam," Cheryl called after him. She unbuckled the last strap and pulled her foot out. Sharp needles of pain stabbed through her instep as she stood. Gritting her teeth, she began to walk back and forth testing her strength and balance. Another groan from the old timbers of the building caused her to look up in fear. She heard the twins calling, and she stepped up to the gaping hole in the wall.

"Are you coming, Cheryl?" Kayla called.

"You bet I am, sweetheart. I'll come right over."

"Hurry, please. I'm cold," Lindy called.

"It won't be long now," Cheryl promised.

Sam returned with a coiled rope. "If I can get this over one of those rafters, I'll be able to hold you up if you fall." He gave a pointed look at her bare feet. "How's the foot?"

"Okay."

"Are you sure?" He made a toss with the rope and missed.

"I'm sure."

The next toss of the rope went over the

exposed rafter. He caught the dangling end and jerked on it. The beam held.

He turned to her and held out a loop. "Put this around your waist." She did, and he tightened it, then gathered up the slack. "Ready?"

She nodded and carefully tested the beam in front of her. "I think it will hold, but I'm going to need some way to secure them to me so I can have my hands free for balance."

Sam pulled a small pocketknife from his jeans, cut a length of rope from his end, and handed it to her. She knotted it and slipped it over her head and one shoulder, then she stepped out onto the beam with her arms raised from her sides and concentrated on finding her center of balance.

The beam under her bare feet was only about three inches wide. "Now I remember why I didn't become a gymnast," she muttered under her breath as she took several steps. Her ankle felt weak and wobbly, but it would hold. It had to.

She looked at the small faces huddled together across the church, and she began to walk toward them with a smile set firmly on her face.

Gusts of wind pushed at her back like a giant hand and whipped her hair across her eyes to blind her. The old beam beneath her bare feet was rough with splinters. In places, it was wet and slippery from the rain that poured in through the hole in the roof. Each flash of lightning illuminated the danger that lay below her.

The sharp tines of a rusting, rain-slicked harrow gleamed dully in one flash, the grimy panes of a shattered window reflected her above it in the next one. She took each step with careful determination until she reached the jumble of boards where the twins sat.

"Stay still until I tell you to move. I can only take one of you at a time, so who wants to go first?" She turned around and lowered herself to straddle the beam at the edge of the fallen piece of roof.

"Lindy can go," Kayla offered. She scooted back and made more room for her sister. Bonkers climbed into Kayla's lap, and she clutched him tightly.

"Okay, good. Lindy, I want you to put your

arms and legs around me and hold on tight. I'm going to tie this rope around us to help hold you on."

"I can't. I'm scared."

"I know you are, but I won't let anything bad happen to you. Your daddy can hold us up if we fall."

Lindy shook her head and whispered, "I can't."

"Okay, this is what I want you to do. I want you to close your eyes. Can you do that?"

"I guess so."

"But first, put your arms around my neck."

"Okay. But Cheryl, I'm not sleeping."

Cheryl tied the rope around them both.

"Now, I've got a job for you. I want you to keep your eyes closed tight. Can you do that?"

"Yes."

Lindy did as she was told, and Cheryl stood carefully. She looked back at Kayla's pale face. "I'll be right back for you."

"Promise you won't leave me?"

Cheryl felt a lump rise in her throat. "I'm not going to leave you, baby. I'll be right back. I promise."

It was difficult to keep her balance with Lindy's added weight, and Cheryl's foot hurt with every step. She glanced once at Sam's worried face.

"You're doing fine," he coaxed. "Only a few more steps."

It took five more steps before Cheryl grasped Sam's strong hand, and he pulled her to solid ground. Quickly, he untied the small rope and shifted Lindy to his arms. The rain poured down in torrents, and the old building shuddered in the fierce wind.

"Hurry," he said as he set Lindy on the ground and pulled the slack out of the rope.

Cheryl stepped back onto the beam and tried to do just that. She lost her balance and wobbled wildly for an instant before she steadied herself.

Behind her, she heard Sam's reassuring voice. "Easy, girl, easy. Are you okay?"

"Just peachy," she said through clenched teeth as she waited for her bounding pulse to settle.

"You can do it, I know you can."

"I'm fine." She took a deep breath and began to walk toward Kayla and Bonkers.

When she reached the edge of the boards again, she smiled at Kayla. "I told you I'd be back. You and I are going to do the same thing, okay?" She sat down. "Climb on."

A sharp report sounded above their heads, followed by a grating groan that shook the boards they sat on. Cheryl glanced up, then quickly twisted around to cover Kayla's small body with her own as a shower of wooden shingles rained down from a new hole in the roof. A long piece of a splintered rafter fell, stabbing through the flimsy wood inches away from her head.

"Are you okay?" Sam's frantic voice filled the sudden silence.

"We're okay." Cheryl sat up with Kayla clutched tightly in her arms.

"Well, get out of there! This whole place is about to come down," he yelled.

"I'm not dawdling in here because I want to!" she shouted back. Another loud crack rent the air. The rafter holding her safety rope snapped in two and fell into the cellar.

Cheryl stared at the useless rope. Kayla tugged at her arms. "I'm cold. Can we go now?"

Cheryl looked down at the face of the child she loved with all her heart. "Yes, honey. Let's go home, shall we?" She threw off the useless safety line and stood.

"Come on, girls. I know you can do it."

Cheryl heard the controlled fear in Sam's voice. She shifted Kayla to her back and tightened the small rope around them. Bonkers dashed out onto the beam in front of them. He trotted a little way out, then turned around to see if they were following. He ran the rest of the way, jumped out and stood with flattened ears in the rain.

"Show off," Cheryl muttered as she started walking.

Another sharp crack split the air. The beam under Cheryl's feet quivered wildly and shifted, and she gave a cry of alarm. A piece of falling shingle hit her head, and she struggled to maintain her balance as the beam under her dropped several inches.

Righting herself, Cheryl looked at Sam, and her heart skipped a beat before it began to thud in fear. He lay facedown, holding on to the splintered end of beam she stood on. The veins in his neck stood out as he held their combined weight and the heavy beam. She began to walk quickly, hoping he could hold them up.

Suddenly, a series of powerful reports rent the air. An ominous moaning started low, then grew louder and louder.

"Jump!" Sam yelled.

Cheryl leaped toward the opening as the beam gave way behind her. She knew she wasn't going to make it. She landed half in and half out of the opening. She felt Kayla's weight pulling her backward as she clawed for a handhold in the wet grass.

In an instant, Sam's strong hands clamped on to her arms, and he pulled her up beside him. They scrambled to their feet and ran as the roof caved in and the ends of the church toppled inward with a deafening crash.

As suddenly as it started, the sounds died away. Cheryl clung to Sam as they stood looking at a pile of wreckage where the old church had stood. With trembling hands, she began to untie the rope at her waist. Sam lifted Kayla from her back and gave the child a quick hug. "Are you okay?" he asked.

"Yes, Daddy."

He kissed her cheek, then set her on the ground.

"I want to go home," Lindy said.

"That's a very good idea," Cheryl agreed.

Sam grasped her arm. "Thank you. I don't know what I would have done without you."

"I'm cold," Kayla said with a shiver.

"Can we go?" Lindy asked.

"Bonkers doesn't—"

"—like the rain."

"He wants—"

"—to go home, too."

"Of course." Cheryl turned away and herded the girls toward the truck.

The twins told them what had happened as they drove back to the ranch.

"The man said he was going to Wichita," Kayla began after she exchanged looks with her sister.

"We decided to go and wait there for you," Lindy admitted.

"Then you'd have to bring us home, and you could stay some more."

"We were in the dark a long time." Lindy's voice grew dramatic.

"And we didn't like it," Kayla added.

"The truck stopped, and we thought maybe it was Wichita, so I opened the door to see and—"

"—Bonkers jumped out."

"We got out to catch him but—"

"—the truck drove away and left us."

"It started to rain, and Bonkers ran into the church. The door wouldn't open very far, but we got in."

"Bonkers ran over some boards to a dry place, and we followed him. Then the boards fell down, and we couldn't get out," Kayla finished in a rush.

Sam shook his head. "This was the most harebrained idea you've ever cooked up. You're grounded till you're twenty-one."

"But, Dad!"

"Two weeks, and I don't want to hear another word."

Sam used his cell phone to call the ranch to let his mother and grandfather know that the twins were safe. Eleanor and Walter were waiting when he drove into the ranch yard. Cheryl recognized her sister's green Mazda parked in front of the house. Eleanor knelt down, and the girls ran to throw their arms around her in a big hug.

"Hi—"

"—Grandma."

"You girls scared me to death," she scolded.

"We're—"

"—sorry."

Walter watched them with an indulgent smile. He looked at Cheryl and said, "Your brother told the sheriff about the Double R cowboy who was looking for help to heist some cattle. His tip paid off."

"You found Harvey?" Cheryl's sadness lifted a little as he nodded. At least Sam had a chance now to get the ranch back on its feet.

"Apparently, he tried to sell them in his hometown just outside of Emporia. He had a forged bill of sale, but it seems he didn't have an explanation for why his bull had rose-pink toenails. The sale barn operator got suspicious and notified the law."

Eleanor gave the twins a small push in Walter's direction. "Take them in the house and get them cleaned up, will you?"

He nodded and took each girl by the hand.

"Come and tell Grandpa all about it. How long are you grounded for?"

"Two whole weeks," Lindy admitted with a long face.

"That's not bad. Did I ever tell you about the time I got grounded for a whole year?" His voice trailed off as he led the girls into the house.

Eleanor faced Cheryl. "Your sister is here," she said just as Angie stepped out onto the porch.

Sam came up beside Cheryl. "You're leaving now?"

"Yes."

She waited for him to speak, to ask her to stay, but he didn't. She forced a smile to her face. "I'm glad you'll get your cattle back, and I'm glad the girls are safe, and I'm sorry—about everything." She turned and hurried to her sister's car, determined that no one would see how much her heart was breaking.

Sam watched her go. He'd been so wrong about her. He'd let his festering pain and anguish over his wife's deceptions keep him from seeing the truth about her. He loved

Cheryl, but at the first test of that love, he'd failed her miserably.

Her sister stopped in front of Sam and held out her hand. "Thanks for taking care of Cheryl."

Sam took her hand and nodded mutely.

Angie glanced toward the car where Cheryl sat with her head bowed, then back at him. "Oh, come on. You're not really going to let her go, are you?"

"She doesn't want to stay."

"You can't be that stupid." She eyed him for a long moment, then shook her head. "I guess you can." She started to walk away, but stopped and turned back to him. "She loves you, you know."

Sam's gaze moved to where Cheryl sat quietly in the car with her head up staring straight ahead. "She never told me that."

"Men. Do women have to tell you everything? Cheryl is the bravest and most loyal person I know, and you're a fool if you let her go."

She walked down the steps and joined her sister.

His mother laid a hand on his arm. "Are you okay, son?"

"You heard her. I'm a fool." Sam watched them drive away and swallowed the lump in his throat. "She's the wrong kind of woman for me. Her career will take her all over the world. She said herself that she doesn't have time for a family, or children. Yet, today, she risked everything for Lindy and Kayla. She's the wrong kind of woman in every way, except she's the only woman who can fill my heart and my life. And I just let her go."

"What are you going to do?"

"I don't know, Mom. I just don't know."

She reached up and cupped his face between her hands. "You'll figure it out, Sam. I know you will."

"I don't see how you can be so sure."

"Your mother didn't raise no fool."

Chapter Seventeen

Cheryl completed a single pirouette on her left foot and frowned. Dressed in a leotard and toe shoes, she worked out in her sister's spare bedroom.

"Does it hurt?"

Cheryl looked up and smiled at Angie in the doorway. "Not much, but it's weak."

"You should give it a rest."

"I can't." She rose on her toes again. "I have an audition in two weeks, and I need to be ready."

"Jeff and I are going out to dinner tonight. Why don't you join us?"

"No, thanks." Cheryl began another spin.

Angie walked up and stopped her by putting both hands on her shoulders. "If he hasn't called by now, he isn't going to."

Cheryl bowed her head. "I know," she admitted.

"You can call him. The phone works in both directions."

The doorbell rang, and Angie frowned at the interruption. She gave her sister a firm shake. "Go back to him or go on with your life, but don't stay in limbo."

Cheryl stared at the phone on the bedside table. It had been two weeks, and every day she had hoped for some word from Sam, but she'd heard nothing. Did she dare call him? Her sister was right—she had to go back to him and try again, or get on with her life.

She couldn't imagine her life without Sam and the girls in it. She had to give it one more chance. She took a deep breath and reached for the phone, but stopped at the sound of her sister's laughter.

"Well it's about time," Angie said. "What took you so long?"

"We've been grounded."

"For two whole weeks."

"It was really bad!"

"No TV—"

"—or nothin'!"

Cheryl dashed into the room and froze as a wave of happiness spread over her. Sam stood in her sister's living room, looking nervous and uncertain. When he saw her, that endearing, crooked grin appeared on his handsome face.

The twins stood on either side of him. Kayla held a bouquet of roses she could barely see over, and Lindy held a giant, red, heart-shaped box of chocolates. Bonkers sat in front of them. He wore a bright-red ribbon tied around his neck with the other end firmly knotted to Sam's wrist.

Sam smiled at her. "You said the next time I wanted to get you to come home with me, I would have to promise you chocolate and roses."

Tears of happiness stung her eyes as she walked up to him and laid her hands on his chest. "My price has gone up since then, cowboy."

"Oh? What'll it take now?"

"I won't settle for anything less than a cowboy, two kids and a cat."

"That can be arranged." He gathered her into his arms and kissed her with such fierce longing, it stole her breath away.

He drew back and studied her face. "When Natalie left me, she left a hole big enough for Harvey to walk though. I didn't know if I could ever trust my heart to another woman again. Then you came into my life, and before I knew it, you had mended my heart.

"I've done a lot of soul searching in the past two weeks. It wasn't that I couldn't trust anyone else, it was that I didn't trust myself. If I had been more open, less worried about getting hurt, you might have been able to confide in me."

"I'm so sorry, Sam. It was a mistake I'll never make again. I don't deserve your love, but I love you with all my heart."

"You deserve a better man than me. And I'm going to spend a lifetime trying to become that man. I don't want you to give up ballet," he said sternly. "You can go anywhere in the world to work as long as you come home to us."

"Ask her, Daddy," Lindy urged.

"Yeah, ask her," Kayla added.

Motioning to them with one hand, he said, "Just wait a minute."

He looked back at Cheryl. "The girls and I understand we're going to have to share you. We're prepared for that. I only hope ballerinas make good money because the airfare back and forth to New York is going to cost us a bundle."

"Do you think I'm worth it?" she asked with a shy grin.

He pulled her close. "Oh, yes."

"Ask her, Daddy," Kayla insisted.

Cheryl forced her face into a serious pose. "Ballerinas don't make that much money. I think all I'll be able to afford is the gas to Kansas City and back."

"What do you mean?"

She smiled broadly. "I have an audition with a ballet company in Kansas City next month."

She grew serious as she studied his face. "It will mean I'll be away working—sometimes for weeks at time. It won't be easy, Sam."

"I know." He smoothed her hair with his

fingertips. "But it can't be as hard as life without you. I tried that for the past two weeks. It didn't work. I'll support you in anything you want to do."

"I want to perform for at least another two years, then I want to do something else."

"Anything. I'll never stand in your way."

"I want to teach. I want to start a dance school in Council Grove."

"I like the sound of that."

"Ask her, Dad."

"Yeah, ask her."

Cheryl grinned down at the girls. "Okay, ask me what?"

"To marry him," Lindy blurted out.

"And be our mother," Kayla added.

Sam rolled his eyes and shook his head. "Like they said—will you marry me?"

"In a New York minute. I love you, Sam." She cupped his face and kissed him with all the love she held in her heart.

The twins grinned at each other and winked.

Bonkers began to purr, but no one noticed as he wound the red ribbon around and around their boots and ballet shoes.

* * *

In the little dressing room at the back of the stone church on the outskirts of Council Grove, Cheryl Steele planted her hands on her hips. "This veil is crooked. I can't possibly wear it."

"Hush," Angie said. "Come here and let me fix it. There."

Cheryl turned around. "Well? How do I look?"

"You look…radiant…beautiful…. I don't think I can find the right words. Sam is a very lucky man. I hope he knows it."

A mischievous grin curved Cheryl's lips. "He does. I tell him every chance I get."

Angie chuckled. "I'll bet you do."

Cheryl reached out and grasped her sister's hands. "Have I ever thanked you?"

"For what?"

"For pushing me into going back to the ranch that night?"

Angie leaned close. "I've never asked, but was it hard for you?"

"You mean facing the community and telling people who I am? Yes, and no. But with Sam and his family around me, it turned into a healing time.

"Over the past few months so many people have come up to me and talked about Mom. A lot of people felt they let her down. Spousal abuse wasn't talked about back then. Things have changed. For the better."

"Do you think they'll accept Jake?"

"Yes, in time. The sheriff made it known that Jake was the one who solved the theft of Sam's cattle. There will always be people with prejudices against an ex-con, but there are enough people here who believe he deserves another chance. With Walter Hardin as his outspoken supporter, Jake has a good shot at it."

"And Doris? I noticed she wasn't here?"

"Doris and I are trying to mend fences. That may take a while. She wants to shut herself away from the world. I know how that feels, but I haven't given up on her. Listen to me, I sound like a rancher's wife already. Mending fences."

"I knew those New York roots weren't as deep as you pretended."

"I guess they weren't."

A knock sounded at the door and Angie went to open it. Jake stood on the other side. Cheryl had chosen him to walk her down the aisle. His guitar rested in the front pew. She wasn't about to get married without his beautiful music as part of the ceremony. He looked at once handsome and uncomfortable in his rented tux.

He cleared his throat and pulled at the collar of his outfit with one finger. "Are you ready?"

Two little girls in matching floor-length lavender dresses pushed in past his legs. "Come on, Cheryl. We're ready," they said together. Each one grabbed her hand and tugged.

"Daddy is so nervous."

"I wish Bonkers could be here."

"Don't we look nice?"

"Did you see Aunt Becky's baby?"

"He's so cute. Grandma says—"

"—we might get a baby brother, too."

"Maybe even twins, like us!"

Cheryl let herself be led from the room by the excited pair. At the doorway, she cast a wide-eyed look back at her sister. "What have I gotten myself into?"

Angie laughed softly. "Well, get going and find out."

* * * * *

REQUEST YOUR FREE BOOKS!

2 FREE INSPIRATIONAL NOVELS
PLUS 2
FREE
MYSTERY GIFTS

REQUEST YOUR FREE BOOKS!

2 FREE RIVETING INSPIRATIONAL NOVELS
PLUS 2 FREE MYSTERY GIFTS

Love Inspired®
SUSPENSE

YES! Please send me 2 FREE Love Inspired® Suspense novels and my 2 FREE mystery gifts (gifts are worth about $10). After receiving them, if I don't wish to receive any more books, I can return the shipping statement marked "cancel". If I don't cancel, I will receive 4 brand-new novels every month and be billed just $4.49 per book in the U.S. or $4.99 per book in Canada. That's a saving of at least 22% off the cover price. It's quite a bargain! Shipping and handling is just 50¢ per book in the U.S. and 75¢ per book in Canada.* I understand that accepting the 2 free books and gifts places me under no obligation to buy anything. I can always return a shipment and cancel at any time. Even if I never buy another book, the two free books and gifts are mine to keep forever.

123/323 IDN FEHR

Name	(PLEASE PRINT)	
Address		Apt. #
City	State/Prov.	Zip/Postal Code

Signature (if under 18, a parent or guardian must sign)

Mail to the **Reader Service:**
IN U.S.A.: P.O. Box 1867, Buffalo, NY 14240-1867
IN CANADA: P.O. Box 609, Fort Erie, Ontario L2A 5X3

Not valid for current subscribers to Love Inspired Suspense books.

**Are you a subscriber to Love Inspired Suspense
and want to receive the larger-print edition?
Call 1-800-873-8635 or visit www.ReaderService.com.**

* Terms and prices subject to change without notice. Prices do not include applicable taxes. Sales tax applicable in N.Y. Canadian residents will be charged applicable taxes. Offer not valid in Quebec. This offer is limited to one order per household. All orders subject to credit approval. Credit or debit balances in a customer's account(s) may be offset by any other outstanding balance owed by or to the customer. Please allow 4 to 6 weeks for delivery. Offer available while quantities last.

Your Privacy—The Reader Service is committed to protecting your privacy. Our Privacy Policy is available online at www.ReaderService.com or upon request from the Reader Service.

We make a portion of our mailing list available to reputable third parties that offer products we believe may interest you. If you prefer that we not exchange your name with third parties, or if you wish to clarify or modify your communication preferences, please visit us at www.ReaderService.com/consumerschoice or write to us at Reader Service Preference Service, P.O. Box 9062, Buffalo, NY 14269. Include your complete name and address.

REQUEST YOUR FREE BOOKS!

2 FREE INSPIRATIONAL NOVELS
PLUS 2
FREE
MYSTERY GIFTS

Love Inspired
HISTORICAL
INSPIRATIONAL HISTORICAL ROMANCE

YES! Please send me 2 FREE Love Inspired® Historical novels and my 2 FREE mystery gifts (gifts are worth about $10). After receiving them, if I don't wish to receive any more books, I can return the shipping statement marked "cancel". If I don't cancel, I will receive 4 brand-new novels every month and be billed just $4.49 per book in the U.S. or $4.99 per book in Canada. That's a saving of at least 22% off the cover price. It's quite a bargain! Shipping and handling is just 50¢ per book in the U.S. and 75¢ per book in Canada.* I understand that accepting the 2 free books and gifts places me under no obligation to buy anything. I can always return a shipment and cancel at any time. Even if I never buy another book, the two free books and gifts are mine to keep forever.

102/302 IDN FEHF

Name	(PLEASE PRINT)	
Address		Apt. #
City	State/Prov.	Zip/Postal Code

Signature (if under 18, a parent or guardian must sign)

Mail to the **Reader Service:**
IN U.S.A.: P.O. Box 1867, Buffalo, NY 14240-1867
IN CANADA: P.O. Box 609, Fort Erie, Ontario L2A 5X3

Not valid for current subscribers to Love Inspired Historical books.

Want to try two free books from another series?
Call 1-800-873-8635 or visit www.ReaderService.com.

* Terms and prices subject to change without notice. Prices do not include applicable taxes. Sales tax applicable in N.Y. Canadian residents will be charged applicable taxes. Offer not valid in Quebec. This offer is limited to one order per household. All orders subject to credit approval. Credit or debit balances in a customer's account(s) may be offset by any other outstanding balance owed by or to the customer. Please allow 4 to 6 weeks for delivery. Offer available while quantities last.

Your Privacy—The Reader Service is committed to protecting your privacy. Our Privacy Policy is available online at www.ReaderService.com or upon request from the Reader Service.

We make a portion of our mailing list available to reputable third parties that offer products we believe may interest you. If you prefer that we not exchange your name with third parties, or if you wish to clarify or modify your communication preferences, please visit us at www.ReaderService.com/consumerchoice or write to us at Reader Service Preference Service, P.O. Box 9062, Buffalo, NY 14269. Include your complete name and address.

LIH11B

HARLEQUIN® HEARTWARMING™

A TOUCHING STORY ABOUT SECOND
CHANCES AND COMING HOME
FROM AUTHOR

Caron Todd

When Elizabeth Robb left Three Creeks, she never
expected to return. Now that she's back in town,
she hopes her arrival will escape notice. But once
Elizabeth meets Jack McKinnon, she begins to
believe there might be some good to come from
the long journey home. But Jack's got a past,
too—one he'll have to put to rest before he and
Elizabeth can find their future together.

Return To Three Creeks

Coming soon!

Available wherever books are sold.

♦ Harlequin®

HARLEQUIN HEARTWARMING

A special collection of wholesome, tender romances.

Available wherever books are sold!